# Death

## is a

# Blank

# Canvas

By

Ann Sutton

**An invitation-only art exhibition. A rising star cut down in his prime. The only suspects, family and a handful of aristocrats. How will Percy navigate these treacherous waters to solve the callous crime?**

In this gripping sequel, Percy Pontefract finds herself entangled in a twisted web of murder and lies that strikes painfully close to home, when her talented cousin is brutally killed as the curtain rises on his inaugural modern art exhibition in the heart of London.

The shadow of suspicion looms over everyone present; Percy's colorful relatives and a number of enigmatic aristocrats. When circumstances thrust Percy into detection, she is soon caught up in a dangerous game of cat and mouse as she unravels the truth and concludes that the solution to the murder lies beneath layers of paint, privilege and pretension. She must rely on intuition and luck to avoid becoming the next victim.

Set against a backdrop of the glamorous world of fine art and filled with a cast of eccentric characters, Death Is a Blank Canvas, is a rollicking good whodunnit that will keep you guessing until the very end.

*Death is a Blank Canvas is Book 2 in the new Percy Pontefract Cozy Mystery Series.*

Published by

Wild Poppy Publishing LLC
Highland, UT 84003

Distributed by Wild Poppy Publishing

Cover design by Julie Matern
Cover Design ©2023 Wild Poppy Publishing LLC

Edited by Waypoint Authors

Dedicated to Stephen Sutton

## *Style Note*

I am a naturalized American citizen born and raised in the United Kingdom. I have readers in America, the UK, Australia, Canada and beyond. But my book is set in the United Kingdom.

So which version of English should I choose?

I chose American English as it is my biggest audience, my family learns this English and my editor suggested it was the most logical.

This leads to criticism from those in other English-speaking countries, but I have neither the time nor the resources to do a special edition for each country.

I do use British words, phrases and idioms whenever I can (unless my editor does not understand them and then it behooves me to change it so that it is not confusing to my readers).

This manuscript was professionally proofread numerous times. Though I do my best to eliminate all typos and punctuation mistakes, inevitably some will slip through. If you happen to notice one, please send me an email at annsuttonauthor@gmail.com.

Thank you for your understanding.

# Table of Contents

# Chapter 1

Heart in her throat, Percy tentatively raised a gloved hand to wave through the windscreen.

She swiped angrily at a stray tear. She must *not* let the boys see her weeping…that was, if either of them turned around. The raised hand immobile, her wave dead on the vine, she could not seem to drop her arm.

Just as both boys were about to be swallowed by the massive, fort-like school door, William turned, shining on her his beloved, toothy smile and waving madly before his brother shoved him forward. How was it possible to live with your heart cracked in two?

Cheeks damp, she wiped them again as a sleek, silver Rolls Royce Phantom overtook her modest, green Ford in the drop off line. She stared at the hungry, detestable, school door for five more agonizing minutes, frozen in misery.

Finally, summoning her courage, Percy depressed the clutch, threw the car into gear and shuddered away from the front of the loathsome boarding school, hardly able to see the road ahead.

Her attempts to convince her husband, Piers, that there was an eminently suitable day school not twenty minutes from their home had fallen on deaf ears. St. Wilfred's was, and would remain, a family tradition.

*Pooh tradition!*

She had pleaded, begged, whined and wailed, throwing all self-respect to the wind, but Piers had remained unmoved. Besides, as he pointed out, His Majesty's Government was subsidizing the fees.

Resolved to failure on the choice of school, she absolutely refused to give in to the suggestion that the boys should take the train. Alone.

"They might be teased if you drop them off," intoned Piers from behind *The Times*.

"It is a risk I am willing to take," she snapped. "I will *not* be deterred!"

Piers bent the top of the page over, staring at her. "If you insist." The paper resumed its former position.

"I do!" she almost shouted, resisting the urge to throw a piece of toast at the newspaper barricade.

Now, blinded by hot tears, she wondered if she would end up in a ditch on the way home. Perhaps a fond farewell at the train station was preferable after all. *No!* She was their *mother*, and she would see them safely to the school, even if it killed her.

"As bad as all that, was it?" chimed Mrs. Appleby as Percy pushed her way into the friendly kitchen for a comforting piece of warm pie, a cup of tea and a large side of womanly sympathy.

"Worse!" she howled, dropping her expanding bottom into one of the battered kitchen chairs.

"Perhaps Mr. Pontefract was—"

"Stop right there!" bellowed Percy, holding up a hand. "You are my *one* ally, Mrs. A. Don't fail me now."

"As you wish," pronounced Mrs. Appleby, pushing a generous piece of apple pie smothered in custard across the table. "On the bright side, you'll have more time to perfect your sleuthing skills."

Percy growled.

She had recently appeared in court as a witness in the murder and treason trial of two friends. It was her undercover sleuthing that had resulted in their arrest. The pair had both been found guilty, but fortunately, the court had shown mercy in the case of the mother, and she had been sentenced to life in prison. Her accomplice had been sentenced to the noose.

It was not an experience she cared to repeat.

Digging her spoon into the creamy custard and pie as if the dessert had slapped her, she crammed the loaded utensil into her mouth. The sweet, thick cream and flaky, short-crust pastry dissolved on her tongue, working its magic. She closed her eyes in rapture.

"Your pie can cure many ills, Mrs. A."

"Perhaps I should sell it to members of parliament," said the cook with a chuckle.

For several minutes, Mrs. Appleby busied herself with the dishes, leaving Percy to enjoy her guilty pleasure.

"Oh, the postman came while you were gone and there's a letter for you." Mrs. Appleby pushed the pile of mail toward her. Percy flicked through with little interest until she came to a thick, linen envelope sealed with a red wax stamp. *Who on earth would be sending her one of these?*

She broke the seal and withdrew a gold-embossed invitation.

*The pleasure of your company*
*is requested*
*at the*
*private*
*Opening Gala*
*of*
*The Packett Art Gallery*
*Exhibiting*
*the work of*
*Nigel Fotherington Esq.*
*Chelsea, SW 10*
*January 16, 1928*

Nigel. Her second cousin. She hadn't seen him in years. This was her mother's doing. The only memories she had of Nigel were from when they played *Spin the Bottle* at a Christmas party when she was fourteen and he had planted a wet, slobbery kiss on her unwilling lips. She had wiped it off in disgust. He had teased her relentlessly.

Racking her weary brain, she tried to drum up a memory of her mother mentioning that Nigel had become an artist but came up blank. To be honest, she tuned her mother out most of the time, so it could be that Mrs. Crabtree had often sung his praises and she had not listened.

Percy huffed in indecision. If she accepted, she would be forced to spend time with her mother. But, if she declined, her mother would arrive, badgering her about why she had embarrassed the family. It was a sticky situation.

She stuck out her bottom lip.

"Bad news?" asked Mrs. Appleby, cleaning the draining board with a cloth.

"The worst. I shall have to spend time with Mother."

"Ah." So much pity was infused in the tiny exclamation. During her ten years of working for the Pontefracts, Mrs. Appleby had crossed paths with Mrs. Crabtree on many occasions. Frankly, anyone who had spent more than five minutes with Percy's mother knew what torment it was.

Percy raised the thick card. "It's an invitation to an art gallery opening, featuring the work of a cousin. If I don't go, Mother will come to ask why, so I might as well gird up my loins and accept."

Mrs. Appleby wiped off the tabletop with a wet cloth. "Could be fun. Rubbing elbows with important people, and all."

Percy gasped. "I have absolutely *nothing* suitable to wear. I shall have to order a new dress, and I positively refuse to go shopping with Mother."

4

At almost six feet, Percy was confined in her choices. Off-the-rack designs did not accommodate women of her height. As a consequence, there were only two bespoke dress makers she frequented: one in the next village over, and one in Dorking, about twenty miles away. Still feeling blue about the forced separation from her children, she plumped for Westover's in Dorking—she deserved a restorative cream tea, and Dorking boasted several options.

Standing in her underwear on a small, round platform in the private dressing area of the venerable dressmaker's shop, Percy tried to avoid looking in the full-length mirror. Two pregnancies had certainly left their mark, and her predilection for sugary treats had only added fuel to that particular fire.

"Ready?" asked Miss Kettering, the talented seamstress, through the door.

"Yes," she squeaked.

The vulnerability of being half-naked in the presence of near strangers was akin to being offered up to the gods for slaughter. She was rarely so exposed, even at home, where she hid herself from Piers when she changed. She had resolved to diet countless times, but it never lasted more than a few days.

"Right then." The immaculately dressed Miss Kettering and a young, impossibly thin assistant entered, laden with clipboards and measuring tape. The younger woman threaded an offensive measuring tape under Percy's arms and around her ample chest.

"Forty-two," she sang as Miss Kettering wrote the figure on a document on the clipboard.

*Forty-two inches?* It had been some time since Percy had bought any new clothes, but she was pretty sure that her chest measurement had still been in the thirties. Glad to ditch the old-fashioned corset favored by her mother's generation, Percy preferred the modern, expandable bandeaus which pushed everything in. However, Miss

Kettering had asked that it be removed for the fitting, and everything was falling out.

The tiny assistant reached around Percy's midriff, cheek almost touching her silky slip. "Forty-one."

Again, Percy was shocked and for two whole seconds rethought the cream tea.

Mercifully, instead of reaching around her nether regions, Miss Kettering held one end of the tape while her assistant walked behind.

Percy winced in alarmed anticipation.

"Forty-four!"

Percy's mouth shrugged. Worse than she had hoped.

The assistant took more measurements across her shoulders, down her arms and from shoulder to ankle.

When they were finished, Percy felt quite violated and wrapped her arms around her substantial bust.

"You can put your clothes back on and come through to the main showroom to look through patterns and fabrics," trilled the seamstress.

Percy slunk back to the large changing cubicle and hurriedly re-dressed with a heavy heart. She must have gone up at least two dress sizes in the last five years. She took heart in the fact that, compared to her mother, she was still considered trim.

Miss Kettering had arranged several books of patterns, and Percy sat down to flick through. There were so many styles to choose from. She stopped at a page of sports dresses that had become popular to wear as day dresses. She tried to imagine walking around an art gallery in a tennis dress. No. Not appropriate.

She breezed through pages of shapeless shift dresses. Those only worked for skinny, petite women. She slowed at the picture of a model whose hair had been cut as short as a man's. She reached up to touch her own frizzy locks, tucked into a relatively tidy roll at the neck. Even though her hair was a menace to style, she could not understand how any woman could cut off her crowning glory.

Losing hope, Percy turned the last page and beheld a simple dress, loose knit at the top with subtle beading at the neckline. It had a flowing chiffon skirt and matching, long, puffy sleeves. The dress in the picture was scandalously short, but she was sure she could ask for it to be made to mid-calf. It was paired with a becoming, fashionable, slouch cap which would be useful if she was having a bad hair day—which, frankly, was almost every day.

"How about this one?" she called

Miss Kettering tottered over. "Very nice. May I ask the occasion?"

"It's for the opening of an art gallery and I know the artist."

Miss Kettering cocked a finely plucked brow. "Evening?"

"No, two o'clock in the afternoon."

"Then this is perfect, madam."

After choosing two swatches of complementary burgundy fabrics and explaining her penchant for a longer skirt, Percy paid the deposit and made an appointment for a fitting the following week.

Outside on the pavement, her stomach roared. Bearing right, she entered her favorite tea shop and ordered a full cream tea for one.

Just as she was about to take the first delicious bite, the bell over the door to the tea shop rang and Percy dropped the scone.

*Mother!*

# Chapter 2

Drat her predictability! Why hadn't she chosen an unexpected tea shop?

Percy's first instinct was to hide under the table, but eyeing the dainty looking piece of furniture, she decided it was not feasible. Instead, she stared at the fallen scone praying for invisibility.

"Persephone!"

Her mother's voice was a cross between a foghorn and a dying cow. Percy looked up, hoping the movement of her lips resembled a smile, as the plump woman bounced on her tiptoes across the feminine tearoom. Though hats had become tighter to the head over the last couple of decades, Mrs. Crabtree's was likely to develop its own solar system. Percy watched it nudge several unsuspecting patrons as her mother passed.

"Darling! It's been an age." Her mother was given to overstatement. It had been exactly two weeks since they had seen each other. Two blessed weeks.

Leaning down to kiss her daughter's cheek, Mrs. Crabtree realized her colossal hat would prevent close contact and instead kissed the air.

The antique chair groaned beneath her mother's weight, and Percy allowed herself the luxury of imagining the legs surrendering, causing her mother to tumble backward to the ground.

"What are we having?" Mrs. Crabtree asked, her beady eyes on the scones and clotted cream on Percy's plate.

The words, *Isn't it rather obvious?*, sprang to Percy's tongue, but she stuffed a piece of scone in to stop them in their tracks. After all these years, she knew her mother's rhetorical questions needed no answer. The overbearing woman raised a pudgy hand at a passing waitress. "I say! I say! Can I get some service?"

8

The poor girl had just taken the order of a pair of elderly, identical twins, but it took a strong personality to brush off her mother.

"Uh, yes, I suppose so." The girl was no more than sixteen and no match for Mrs. Crabtree.

"What is today's special?" her mother demanded.

"Fresh strawberry tart and bread pudding." The young waitress turned to a new page in her notebook, a sour look on her pale face.

"I'll take the strawberry tart. And I want Darjeeling tea, not over steeped, with cream and a bowl of sugar."

"Yes, ma'am."

The girl hurried away, and Percy wished she could join her.

"So," began Mrs. Crabtree, removing her gloves. "You're buying a new dress. You should have asked me to come. You know you have the worst taste in clothes."

This was rich coming from a woman wearing birds on her hat and a hideous lime-green coat. Percy would need to have a word with Mrs. Appleby about confidentiality. She sucked in her cheeks before replying.

"I didn't want to bother you, and I was in need of consolation, since the boys returned to school yesterday."

Mrs. Crabtree waved her short arms. "Consolation? Isn't it rather a time for celebration?"

That one sentence summed up her mother's attitude to parenting nicely.

As a child, Percy had spent much more time with nannies and schoolteachers than she ever had with her mother. Then, as she entered the teenage years, everything had changed, and her mother had clung to her like a barnacle but only as an object upon which to lavish her criticism.

Percy's brother, Cedric, had managed to spend as much time away from home as possible, spending summers with school chums and even finding invitations for Christmas,

9

leaving adolescent Percy alone with her mother. She had never forgiven him.

Percy was fond of her formerly outgoing, brow-beaten father, but he was no match for her mother either. Over the years he had slowly transformed into an inanimate object who merely nodded and hummed. He was not a dependable ally.

"*I* am rather fond of my children, Mother, and I feel their loss sorely."

Mrs. Crabtree flicked her napkin in the air and placed it on her capacious knee. "You just need to find more hobbies," she honked. "Like bridge or serving on charitable boards and such." She looked around. "Where *is* that girl?" No one could stand between Mrs. Crabtree and her appetite.

She snapped her attention back to Percy. "I'm devastated that you have chosen a frock without consulting me."

Her mother divided her interactions with Percy into being embarrassed by her tall daughter, and wanting to control all her decisions. Percy's choices, she reasoned, were a reflection on Mrs. Crabtree—they would either elevate her in the eyes of society or shame her.

"I managed quite well alone," Percy said as she took a long sip of fortifying tea.

"What color did you choose?" Her mother's flabby lips were pressed flat in anticipation of hurling sharp criticism. It was her favorite pastime.

"Burgundy." Percy closed her eyes waiting for the onslaught.

"With *your* coloring? Whatever made Miss Kettering agree to that? She should have advised you against a hue that would drain the little color present in your complexion."

It actually didn't matter what color Percy had chosen. Her mother would have found a problem with the whole spectrum in some way or another.

"Miss Kettering thought it a bold choice for an occasion such as an art gallery opening."

"Bold!" Mrs. Crabtree bellowed. "Bold!" All eyes were on her, just as she had calculated. Percy, on the other hand, wanted to crawl under the table again. "I should say it was the *wrong* choice," continued her mother loudly.

"Well, it is *my* choice, Mother," defended Percy. "And that is an end to it." It had taken Percy many years and many tears to learn to stand her ground.

Her mother's wide mouth pinched tight in disapproval and her bountiful chest heaved, but Percy was saved from further injury by the fortunate reappearance of the skinny waitress bearing a strawberry tart.

"So, Nigel is an artist?" Percy began, to steer the conversation away from the deficiencies of her wardrobe.

"Yes, remember? I told you about him a couple of years ago. Cousin Agatha's son. I thought they were throwing good money after bad when he declared his intent to study art, but he has proven quite a phenomenon, it seems. Uggh!" Her mother barely refrained from spitting out the tea. "*Not* Darjeeling!"

Percy let out a puff of air through clenched teeth. Nothing was ever right.

"What kind of art does he do? Oils? Watercolors? Sculpture?"

Her mother's sludge green eyes jerked up. "Do you not listen to a word I say?"

Percy wisely concluded that the truth was not required on this occasion.

Her mother waved a hand around. "He's a *modern* artist, whatever that means."

For the first time since her mother had entered the tea shop, Percy felt her spirits rise. Her mother had no idea what modern art was, and she wasn't about to warn her. Mrs. Crabtree's reaction on arrival at the exhibit would provide some much-needed entertainment.

"Really?"

Suspicion pattered across her mother's broad and pendulous face. "What does *that* mean?"

Percy must be careful not to spill the beans or it would spoil any fun she might anticipate. "Nothing at all. I shall look forward to viewing it. Who else is going?"

"Cousin Agatha, of course. Cecily, his sister. You remember her? She's recently married, though I certainly didn't get an invitation." Mrs. Crabtree sniffed. "Your brother has been invited, though I doubt he will make the effort. My sister Honoria and her worthless husband. I think that's it for family. Agatha assured me there will be several other *important* people."

Mrs. Crabtree had spent a lifetime trying to break out of the middle-class circumstances to which birth had trapped her. To that end, she was always on the alert for the sighting of a peer. This was the real reason for her enthusiasm.

Having been brought up in the same austere household, Aunt Honoria was a carbon copy of her mother. But unlike her mother, Honoria had been forced into an arranged marriage by their ambitious parents. It had proved a disaster. As a consequence, her aunt was unfulfilled and bitter, and the blighted union had never produced offspring.

Percy sighed. Why couldn't Piers for once take time off and accompany her, providing a buffer between herself and her prickly relatives?

"Are you even listening?" demanded her mother.

Percy looked up, completely unaware of her mother's current topic of conversation. Mrs. Crabtree was staring at a woman who had just entered, dressed in the latest fashion with a slouch cap. Percy deduced that her mother disapproved.

"Oh, yes. Awful."

She had guessed right.

"I can't understand why there is such a profession as fashion designer. Their sole purpose is to mess with things," lamented her mother. "The styles of my youth were far superior to most of the cheap stuff of today, and more modest. Do you know, I saw a woman in a dress that almost showed her knees the other day?" This was a beloved topic, and Percy allowed herself to drift away into her own thoughts as she munched on the remains of her scone. With a little inner giggle, she imagined her mother's face when she saw Percy's own version of that very hat!

# Chapter 3

With more confidence than she had mustered in some time, Percy swept into the art gallery, only stumbling slightly on the threshold. She had tried on the beautiful, burgundy dress the day of delivery and Piers had been impressed. He had gone so far as to say that she deserved new dresses more often.

The *Packett Gallery* had an unimposing black and glass door. Inside, the room was a long and narrow starkly white space with a wall down the middle for the presentation of pictures. Small groups were bunched around different works. Percy had learned that this was a private exhibit for a select group of handpicked people before the public opening the following week.

Percy scanned the room for her mother with the intent of avoiding her until the last possible moment. She snagged some canapés and a flute of champagne and approached the first picture. Lines separated angular features portrayed in various primary colors. It was quite hideous. She smiled like a Cheshire cat.

Sliding to the next picture, she frowned. It could be representing a dog or maybe a cat. How delicious. Her mother must be in Purgatory.

Someone moved into her orbit.

"Nigel!"

In appearance he had improved greatly. He wore his dark, wavy hair a little longer and a neatly clipped beard—the quintessential artist. "Percy. Long time no see."

Her eyes fixed on the picture, she responded, "Indeed."

Nigel motioned with the hand holding his champagne, sending drops of golden liquid cascading to the floor. "What do you think?"

She was not sure whether he really cared about her opinion or if he was merely making small talk. "Faithful to the modern style," she said, carefully.

"Agreed." He dropped his voice. "Can you keep a secret?"

This was unexpected.

She looked left without moving her head. Nigel's lengthy, pointed nose quivered while his rich eyes shone with some hidden secret. Was he drunk already?

"Of course."

"I hate them."

Percy's eyes widened. "What do you mean?"

"What I said. I hate them," he whispered. "But this is where the money is right now, so I paint them. They're pretty easy compared to real art."

Suddenly, Percy liked him very much.

"How do you stand it?" she asked with genuine interest.

"I just look at my bank account," he said with a wry smile. "Hunger is a harsh master."

"What do you *like* to paint?" she pushed.

Glancing over his shoulder to make sure no one was within earshot, he dropped his deep voice even lower. "Seascapes. I love the challenge of capturing the movement of wind and light on the water. But no one wants to buy those. They are my passion project."

"I should like to see them one day," she said quietly as Nigel's mother approached, dressed in a flouncy, pink gown bordered with feathers.

"Percy!" Agatha cried, kissing her on the cheek and almost knocking the glass flute from her hand. "You look amazing! It's been too long!"

It certainly had. They had both put on more than a few pounds. Agatha was her mother's cousin on her father's side, and as a consequence, the two families did not get together much.

"Cecily is here somewhere with her new husband. Did you know he is a barrister and sure to be a KC soon?"

King's Counsel. The rung just below the top of the judicial totem pole. Percy inwardly sighed. She hated this game of 'who has the most prestigious relative' and was not about to be baited. "How nice."

"How old are those boys of yours now?" Agatha asked, her hooked nose and tilted head resembling a curious parrot.

"Eleven and eight. They're at St. Wilfred's."

"We prefer King Alfred's in Sussex," she said, sucking in her cheeks and raising her brows as if schooling were a competition.

"It's a family tradition for the Pontefracts," Percy explained. "I'd rather they go to the day school near home, actually."

"No! Really?" Agatha cried, incredulity threatening to knock her clean over. Or was it the champagne? "You can't really *like* having the children under foot."

Wondering how any children turned out as decent, compassionate human beings these days, Percy replied, "Actually, I do."

If Percy had told her she liked singing opera, naked in the back garden, Agatha Fotherington could not have looked more shocked.

"Agatha, who is this vision?" interrupted a portly man in his seventies, sporting a monocle and paisley cravat. He was staring straight at Percy who had never been called a vision in her life.

"Sir William!" said Agatha, moving aside. "Let me introduce my cousin's daughter, Persephone Pontefract."

The older man's eyebrow pressed down hard on the monocle, causing deep creases along his weathered cheek. He looked her up and down as if she were a defenseless heifer at an auction. "Miss?" he warbled.

She raised a hand to meet his. "*Mrs.* Pontefract."

16

"Oh, I *do* beg your pardon." He laid heavy emphasis on the word 'do' and Percy felt the tickle of a giggle in the back of her throat. She swallowed.

"Sir William is the owner of this stylish little gallery and the financial backer for Nigel," Agatha explained. "We are indebted to him."

"Oh," was all Percy could think to say.

Agatha hurried Sir William away.

"Persephone!" Percy hung her head as Mrs. Crabtree's blaring voice blasted over the genteel occasion. "Persephone! You *must* meet Lord Banbury, the Earl of Banbury."

Nothing could ruin this event for her mother now that she had captured her own earl. He was lucky she was not carrying a shotgun. Gritting her teeth, Percy slapped a smile on her face while casting a sidelong look of horror at her cousin. Nigel had a ridiculous grin on his face. He was clearly enjoying the farce at her expense.

The earl could have been anywhere from forty to sixty years of age with a ring of graying hair around his scalp. He held out a limp hand to kiss hers, and she wasn't sure if she should curtsey. In the end she plumped for a kind of bob with her ankles crossed and started to fall to the left. Nigel graciously caught her, pushing her upright.

"I am so delighted to meet you," the earl said, accentuating his 't's and 's's dramatically.  Percy felt a twitch in her lip.

"Likewise," she replied.

"The earl was just telling me about a trip he took to France where he actually met the father of cubes, Paulo Peaches."

A snort from Nigel revealed that her mother had botched the name, but the earl was all manners. "Indeed. Pablo Picasso. Fascinating man." So many s's! Percy daren't look at her cousin.

"Mother, how do you like Nigel's art?" she asked as she cast a critical eye over her mother's extravagant, purple outfit.

The largest, most insincere smile spread from ear to ear as her mother responded. "It is…surprising."

"I must congratulate you, Mr. Fotherington. You capture M. Picasso's style perfectly," simpered the earl. Her mother began to nod like a sprung Jack-in-the-box, and Percy felt the need for some privacy to relieve her pent-up amusement.

"I have not seen the rest of Nigel's work yet. Would you excuse me?" she said.

"Of course," said the earl. "Your mother is splendid company." Percy briefly wondered what his own mother was like if he found hers entertaining.

She lifted her elbow. "Nigel?"

He took the proffered arm. "I'd be delighted to show you the rest of the collection."

"I told you burgundy would drain your color," sneered her mother quietly as they parted company, effectively piercing her good mood.

*Her opinion is of no consequence. Piers thought you looked wonderful.*

"Your mother doesn't change, does she?" chuckled Nigel.

"Does yours?"

"Touché," he responded, searching the room. "I think there's also a dowager countess here, somewhere."

"Then my mother will think she has died and gone to heaven. She'll have even forgiven your mother for not inviting her to your sister's wedding."

"Did she not? You didn't miss much," he snickered. "Have you met Bernard Partridge soon to be KC?"

Percy grabbed another canapé and a fresh champagne glass from the pimply waiter. "I've not yet had the pleasure."

18

"Then let's remedy that, and you will see that my close relatives are as ridiculous as yours."

Passing Percy's aunt, Honoria, who was deep in conversation with a woman who looked like she had just escaped from the Russian revolution, Nigel guided her to the corner where an enormous, cubist rendition of an elephant hung. At least she thought it was an elephant.

A tall, thin, praying mantis of a man, with a spiffing black mustache and oiled hair, stood next to Nigel's sister Cecily, his gaze focused on the painting.

"Bernie," said Nigel, pushing Percy forward. "Meet my cousin, Percy."

The gaunt man turned startling blue eyes on her. "Bernard. Barrister at the Old Bailey. How do you do?" The ring on his little finger winked as he held up his bony hand to take hers in greeting.

"Very well, thank you."

She turned to the tiny, fragile woman next to him. "Hello, Cecily." Percy leaned to give her petite cousin a kiss on the cheek. "How are you?"

Cecily raised adoring eyes to her husband and sighed. "Super-duper."

Bernard turned to his wife, bestowing on her the look a father might give a well-behaved child. Her translucent skin blossomed under the shadow of his approval. Had Percy ever looked at Piers that way?

"What do you call this one?" asked Bernard in his clipped baritone.

Nigel widened his eyes at Percy before replying. "Elephant."

Percy bit back a smile.

"Oh, I thought you might have chosen something more obtuse," Bernard responded, either not noticing or ignoring the humor his question had inspired.

"I believe the style is obtuse enough. Don't you agree, Percy?" asked Nigel.

Knowing from his earlier admission that this style was merely a golden goose, Percy agreed. "Quite."

She turned away from the ugly picture, directing a question to Cecily. "How long have you been married now?"

Cecily's heart-shaped face expanded into a smile of utter pleasure. "Six glorious months. The *best* six months of my life." Her sickly sweet, lovesick tone was almost too much to bear. "Did you know that Bernard was second chair for a big fraud case? He is well on his way in the world. He's hoping for KC within the year." Cecily took a sip of champagne. "And how is dear Piers?" She looked behind Percy with expectation.

Percy had no time for this particular kind of shallow small talk. Cecily had met Piers twice in her life and yet she called him 'dear'.

"Busy. He's a civil servant and travels a great deal."

This seemed to catch the ear of Bernard who had been gazing at the painting as if trying to come up with something intelligent to say about it. "Civil servant? Do you know which branch?"

Percy frowned. She did not. Piers rarely talked about his work, and she was not particularly interested in the details. But could she admit that? "Oh, this and that. He moves from department to department. Where did you go for your honeymoon?"

"Venice!" gushed Cecily, her button nose wrinkling with pleasure. "The gondolas, the sunsets, the history. There's a reason they call it the city of love. Have you been?"

Between school fees and electric bills there never seemed to be any funds left over for exotic holidays. "No. Never. We holiday in Devon."

"Oh." This clearly did not meet the qualification of a real holiday in Cecily's mind. "Well, perhaps one day."

"Yes, perhaps."

20

"Percy, let me introduce you to the Dowager Countess of Kent," said Nigel, assessing the situation correctly.

He guided Percy away from his saccharine sister.

"Thank you," whispered Percy.

"Not much in that girl's head." His tone was snarky, just as a brother's would be.

"That's not quite fair," Percy protested. "Cecily has risen above me in the world and put her foot in it quite innocently." Percy had plenty of experience in that arena.

"I have to agree since she does not possess the acumen for spiteful calculation. I think that's why Bernie married her. He has an insufferable need to be the only sun in his universe. His requirement for a wife was that she be content to be a mere star, offering him unabashed adoration. Cecily fit the bill. She presents no threat of competition."

Percy swatted his arm with a grin. "Why are siblings so mean to each other?"

They moved on, and Percy caught glances of disfigured representations of bowls of fruit, horses, castles and people. Nigel was nothing if not prolific.

"There are so many," she declared.

"Once you get the hang of the style it's not hard," he admitted. "Paint a few black lines, then slap on garish colors in between and voilà."

Percy could not help but laugh at the lack of pretension her cousin had developed. It was pleasantly unexpected.

"How did you come to exhibit here?" she asked.

"Sir William is an art enthusiast and had a hankering to start a gallery. He heard through the grapevine that I was trying to sell this malarkey and asked if I would consider exhibiting for his opening. And he didn't require me to pay up front to rent the space. Our agreement is that he will take a percentage of my earnings. It was an offer too good to turn down. Frankly, I hope it's the break I've been looking for."

He stopped next to the Russian princess from another era.

"Percy, may I present to you the Most Honorable Caroline, the Dowager Countess of Kent, mother of the current Earl of Kent."

As the length of the title expanded, Percy became more and more self-conscious. She was not in the habit of meeting such lofty people. Placing one foot behind the other she attempted her second curtsey of the afternoon. It went much better than the first, and she managed to stay upright.

"Countess, it is a pleasure to meet you."

The deep folds of the dowager's skin gave a clue to her age, but her carriage was stiff as a much younger woman.

"Percy?" Her raspy voice was decidedly upper-class.

"Short for Persephone. Persephone Pontefract. Our mothers are cousins," Nigel explained. "What do you think of my little exhibition, Countess?"

The grand lady's eyes narrowed to slits. "Are you of a tender temperament, young man?"

"Not particularly," he replied.

"Then you won't mind me telling you that I think this is an affront to art." She waved a decorative cane at the distorted picture of a soldier.

Percy was horrified at her temerity, but Nigel began to chuckle. "Not much gets past you, does it, Countess?"

The dowager's steel gray eyes widened in surprise.

"However," he continued. "I would appreciate it very much if you would keep that opinion to yourself this afternoon. I'm hoping to pay my living expenses for the next twelve months from the proceeds of this exhibit. But I would be honored if you would come to see my private collection of more *traditional* artwork."

She lowered her crackly voice. "Do you mean to tell me that you, the artist, do not like this rubbish, yourself?"

"You are correct," he confessed. "But society has crowned this style with its approval and so people are loathed to admit they do not like it. Their snobbery lines my pockets, therefore I produce what the pretenders demand."

The wrinkles re-arranged themselves into a papery smile. "I like you very much Mr. Fotherington. I may just make a purchase and gift it to my intolerable son."

"That would make me very happy, Countess."

The esteemed lady shuffled away chuckling under her breath as Percy's aunt, Honoria Longdale, and her uncle Frederick, slid into their path.

"Was that the Dowager Countess of Kent?" Excitement rippled off her mother's sister bringing color to her mottled cheeks.

"It was," confirmed Nigel.

"W-would you be able to introduce us? I've been watching her for the last half an hour but could not work up the courage."

"I'd be delighted," said Nigel.

Left alone, Percy looked around the select group. She watched with interest as her mother continued to bend Lord Banbury's ear. He looked like a man sentenced to imprisonment, darting glances, searching for an escape. Mrs. Crabtree, on the other hand, would be giddy from all the time spent in the company of aristocrats. The experience would provide her with conversation fodder for years to come.

Percy trained her unprofessional eye on the hideous paintings. She tried to imagine one in her shabby farmhouse but failed. Perhaps when she saw his more traditional work, she might support him by purchasing one.

The afternoon champagne was beginning to affect her. Suddenly light-headed, she fought against the strange urge to chortle. Stopping the waiter, she grabbed another hors-d'oeuvre in the hopes of soaking up some of the alcohol in her stomach. Smoked salmon and caviar—two of her favorites. She grabbed three and the young waiter grinned, stretching his pocked skin into a pleasant smile.

Popping them into her mouth she saw that Nigel was in a heated conversation with Sir William and vaguely wondered if something was wrong. Her mother still had the earl in her clutches, and Cecily and Bernard had moved to the other end of the room.

Feeling her equilibrium disappear, she searched around for a chair.

Finding one in a corner, Percy slumped down, eyes heavy with boozy fatigue. She was not used to drinking in the afternoon. Frankly, she was not used to drinking at all. Stifling a yawn, she attempted to focus on the other guests. The dowager, having managed to escape her aunt, had found another chair and was dozing. Percy looked around for her aunt and uncle but could not see them. Nigel had extricated himself from Sir William's grasp and was heading toward the back of the gallery, no doubt to enjoy a few minutes on his own. A familiar shriek from the other end of the gallery caught her attention. Her mother was gripping the earl's arm, laughing too loudly. Percy felt a responsibility to rescue the poor man, but her body felt incredibly heavy, like she was drowning in mud.

Where was Nigel? She would ask for his assistance. Honoria and Frederick came back into view, her aunt's face flushed, rushing toward her sister.

She would just close her eyes for one minute.

A piercing scream split the air, jerking Percy awake. Her tongue felt bloated and furry. Cecily catapulted into the room from the rear of the building. Her face snow white, she was screaming uncontrollably.

The stick-like figure of her husband hurried to her side. "What is it, my darling?"

She looked up into his angular face, frantic eyes swimming with tears.

"It's Nigel. He's been stabbed!"

# Chapter 4

Cecily's declaration was as effective as a bucket of cold water to Percy's head.

"What?" Percy cried.

"Nigel. In the a-a-alley at the back. H-h-he's...dead." Her wispy cousin collapsed onto the floor before her husband could catch her. Lord Banbury ran past them and into the back of the building as everyone else stood rigid as if locked in time by some macabre magician.

Percy tried to gather her thoughts. Cecily must be wrong. She had just spoken with Nigel. He couldn't be dead.

"Someone call the police!" cried Lord Banbury, sprinting back into the gallery. "Mrs. Partridge is right. Stabbed in the chest. Quick!" He bounded along the back corridor, presumably to stay with the body.

"Don't move him!" called out Percy as the earl disappeared in a flash. "The police don't like it when you move a body," she murmured to the empty hallway.

Her brain began to engage, and she addressed the hesitant waiter, still holding his wares aloft amidst the confusion. "Is there a telephone here?"

"Not yet." He pointed to the front. "But there's a telephone box on the corner."

Percy looked around her. Everyone but Bernard, who was carrying Cecily to a chair in his spindly arms, was still stuck like the poor people of Pompeii.

It was up to her.

Percy rushed to the door, tripping over the mat and out onto the pavement where people were going about their business as if a murder had not just occurred right under their noses. Snapping her head left and right she saw the red box to her left and ran, her capacious handbag swinging wildly from her arm.

A short man in a bowler hat was already in the box. Percy mimed wildly that she had urgent need of the telephone. He cocked an eyebrow, then turned his back to her. *How rude!* She rounded the windowed box and arranged her mild features into an expression of menace. The man narrowed his eyes and turned his back on her again. This reckless disregard for the rule of social manners ignited her anger. She wrenched open the door as the little man looked up at her in horror.

"I need to call the police! There has been a murder!" she bellowed.

"Betty, I need to go," he said meekly, and hung up the phone, muttering to himself, as Percy pushed past him and into the cubicle.

"Hello? Hello?"

"Where can I direct your call?" asked a bored, monotone voice.

"Police! Murder! Police!" Her head was scrambled.

"Murder the police?" asked the telephone operator. "I don't know what kind of—"

Percy cut her off. "There has been a murder." She tried to remember where she was. "Chelsea, SW 10, Ormond St. The Packett Art Gallery."

The operator perked up. "Can you repeat the address, please?"

Percy repeated it. "Hurry!" she said as she slammed the receiver back. She flung open the door and flew out, almost knocking over an old lady holding a scruffy, gray dog.

She grabbed the woman by the arms to prevent her fall. "I'm terribly sorry." The gray-haired woman stared at her in confusion as Percy turned and fled like a hound chasing a rabbit. The pavement had far more people walking on it than a few minutes earlier, and Percy had to navigate her ungainly feet through the flow. She was grateful she had made the new dress longer than the pattern suggested.

Yanking open the door of the gallery, it was evident that people had finally begun to move. Her mother was comforting Agatha as she wept but found time to fix a withering glare on Percy's head. She reached up to find that her slouch hat had fallen back and pulled it forward.

"The police are on their way," Percy explained to the room in general. "I shall see if Lord Banbury needs any assistance."

The first boost of adrenaline-fueled energy had run dry, and she felt herself droop. The bleak reality that her cousin had been murdered hit her like a blow to the back of the head. She had found the grown-up version of her cousin to be someone she would like to get to know. He had matured into a good-humored, agreeable fellow. She felt the loss deeply. Hand outstretched, she braced herself against the wall, trying to regulate her breathing.

A flashback of finding the dead body at Christmas brought a wave of nausea. Would seeing a relative brutally murdered make the experience a thousand times worse? She hobbled to the back of the building, heart in her throat. The corridor narrowed, passed a small kitchen and ended in a slim, windowless, wooden door that stood ajar. Bracing herself, she seized the handle and stepped outside, keeping her eyes up.

"Lord Banbury. I wanted to let you know that the police have been called. Do you need anything?"

The earl's eyes traveled south to the body and, as if pulled by a powerful magnet, her own followed. Nigel was on his side, facing toward her, a knife protruding from his chest, a pool of blood spreading on the ground. His lifeless face gray and waxy. Percy's legs promptly turned to jelly, her vision swimming dangerously. She grabbed the brick wall and looked away.

"I say! Are you alright?" asked the earl. "I think you should go back inside. I'm used to this sort of thing from the war. Ghastly business, but I shall be fine."

Percy clutched at the door handle, pulling ineffectively until she realized she needed to push, then stumbling through into the narrow hall. Once the door was closed, she leaned her back against it, sucking in great gulps of air to settle her queasy stomach, regretting the champagne and caviar.

After a few minutes, Percy managed to stagger back into the main gallery. Bernard was fanning a wan, unconscious Cecily, and Percy's mother was handing Cousin Agatha a handkerchief. Their lives would never be the same.

The dowager sat stone faced, hands atop her cane. Was she angry to be embroiled in a scandal? Back to the wall, Sir William had aged ten years, agitated eyes sagging at the corners. How would this tragedy affect the success of his gallery?

Percy scanned the room for her aunt and uncle. They had retreated to a back corner like mice scurrying into the dark, clinging to each other.

Percy closed her eyes and tried to find her calm. At some point she would need to contact Mrs. Appleby, as there was every possibility she would not make it home for dinner and she did not want her to worry. At least the boys were removed from the horrible event this time. *This time!* What was happening to her ordered life? Was the world going mad? Had someone in this very room stabbed her cousin in broad daylight? As panic began to rise again, she forced it down. Falling to pieces would help no one.

Cecily began to come round, eyes vacant at first. As she remembered the cause of her malaise, she began to wail, producing a morbid background melody. Percy felt her eyes prickle and opened her new handbag to find a handkerchief.

Several minutes passed in this limbo when a distant buzzing began, growing steadily louder until a policeman on a motorcycle pulled up to the curb. In a state of high alert, the bobby pushed into the room.

"Someone reported a murder?" His statement was framed in the tone of a question.

"In the alley," said Percy when no one else spoke. "I can show you." She led the officer down the narrow corridor and showed him to the back door. Rather than leaving, she remained in the hallway keeping the door slightly open in order to hear what Lord Banbury would say.

"And who might you be?" asked the officer.

"Lord Banbury, sixth Earl of Banbury."

Percy bristled. Why did the gentry always wield their titles like weapons?

"I beg your pardon, m'lord." The policeman's authoritative tone had descended a notch or two.

"Quite alright," said the earl in a softer manner.

Percy heard the crack of the officer's knees as he squatted to examine the body.

"Lord Banbury, can you tell me who this is and what has happened here in your own words, please?"

"This is the artist whose work is displayed in the gallery. The group in the room are all special guests invited to a pre-opening reception. The deceased's sister came out here for some reason and found her brother dead on the ground. She screamed before running in to announce his death and then passed out. I rushed back here, as I have some experience with this kind of thing from the war."

"And what is the deceased's name?"

Percy could see the policeman withdraw a notebook through the crack.

"Nigel Fotherington. I do not know his full name."

"And you are here as one of the special guests?"

"I am."

"How were you acquainted with Mr. Fotherington?"

"I wasn't before today. I know Sir William Packett, the owner of the gallery, and he knows I have some interest in Cubist art. The artist is—was an unknown, and Sir William thought the presence of more upper-class members of

30

society might help launch the boy's career. I also have a stake in the *Morning Mail* and was going to write an editorial on the exhibition and send some photographers over tomorrow."

This was all news to Percy.

"Have you moved the body at all?" asked the officer.

"No. You have my word on that," declared Lord Banbury.

"And the body is as you found it, m'lord?"

"Well, there's more blood now, but yes."

Percy's stomach flipped again, and she leaned against the wall, eyes closed.

"Has anyone else been out here to the alley since you came to stand guard?"

"Mrs. Pontefract came out with me at first, but the sight of her cousin stabbed to death understandably made her quite faint."

"Of course," replied the policeman.

"And some of the employees of the other businesses poked their heads out, but I told them to stay put."

Percy heard a slight commotion from the direction of the gallery and slipped into the kitchen, out of sight.

"Can I 'elp you, Missus?"

Percy gasped. *The waiter.* "Oh! No. No, thank you. I am perfectly alright, I just…"

The waiter winked. "That's alright. I was listening too. It'll be our little secret." The young man's hair was too long and needed a wash, but he had a kind face. And now he was a partner in her spying.

Heavy footsteps sounded and dark-blue figures passed the kitchen door. More policemen.

"Dobbins, I need you to stay out here with the body," barked the motorcycle officer. "No one gets back here. No one."

"Alright, Serg," a new voice responded.

31

"Paternoster, you stay in the main gallery and make sure no one leaves."

"Sir!"

"Robnett, I'm posting you outside the front. We're in charge until CID arrives."

"Yessir!" three voices chanted.

*Time to drift back to the gallery.*

Percy disappeared around the door with a nod to the waiter and hightailed it, just before the first policeman arrived to stand guard out front.

"Where have *you* been?" asked her mother in a loud stage whisper.

Percy eyed the officer to see if he had heard. "I was helping the police."

Mrs. Crabtree puckered her lips. "Did you see the…the…Nigel?" It was rare for her mother to be speechless.

"I did," she admitted. "But I wish I hadn't. I keep having horrible flashbacks."

Her mother looked across the room. "Poor Agatha is distraught. Who would do such a thing?"

"That is for the police to determine," replied Percy.

"I can see someone attacking the art," Mrs. Crabtree whispered, but not quietly enough.

"Mother!" Percy whispered back with urgency. "This is not the time to criticize the poor man's work. Show some compassion."

Mrs. Crabtree drew back with a hand to her chest. "You insult me, Persephone. I am the most compassionate person I know."

Percy bit her tongue. Tensions were high. It was no time to get into a difference of opinion with her mother.

"Do you think they will let us leave?" Mrs. Crabtree asked.

"Not until we have all been questioned. A detective is on his way."

32

"Then I shall offer to be questioned first. I have someone coming to dinner tonight."

*So much for the deep well of compassion.*

Percy turned to walk across the room to console Agatha, but the straps of her handbag caught on the back of the chair, and she was tugged back just enough to put her off balance. Her height made it difficult to set sail again and she plumped for sitting in the chair to break her fall. However, her bottom caught the edge and she dropped to the floor, rocking back, legs in the air, like an overturned turtle.

At that very moment, the front door opened, and a tall, handsome man in his forties entered.

"Good afternoon." He looked over at the prostrate Percy with surprise. "I am Chief Inspector Thompson of Scotland Yard, and I will be heading this investigation."

# Chapter 5

Percy's heart sank. What an awful first impression!

Uncle Frederick came to Percy's aid, taking her hand and pulling her up. She kept her eyes firmly away from the barbed judgment of her mother.

The chief inspector rubbed his hands together as he averted his eyes. "Now, who's in charge here?"

Sir William stepped forward. "I am the owner of the gallery, Sir William Packett. I was also Nigel's financial backer."

The chief inspector shook his hand. "I take it that is the name of the deceased."

A sob from Agatha earned a nod from the inspector. "I'll just go and take a look at the crime scene." He turned to depart, then paused. "No one can leave. I'll be back soon to begin the interviews."

Percy's mother raised a hand. "Excuse me, Chief Inspector, but may I be the first to be interviewed? I am a very busy woman and need to get home."

A gasp of incredulity emanated from Agatha that Percy could only attribute to horror at her mother's lack of tact.

The chief inspector's eyes darted from Mrs. Crabtree to Agatha and back. "Sir William, I'll let you organize the order for the interviews, if you wouldn't mind."

*Nice dodge.*

The chief inspector turned on his heel and followed the uniformed police officer to the alley as a gaggle of voices pleaded with Sir William to let them be first.

"Now, now," Sir William began. "I think it would only be proper to let Nigel's mother go first and then his sister." He turned to the dowager. "Countess, I am happy to have you go next, if there is no objection."

Percy peeked at her mother. This was a conundrum wrapped in a dilemma, and the battle warring behind her

34

mother's eyes was plain to see. On the one hand, a knight of the realm was asking Mrs. Crabtree to wait her turn and allow someone far above her in station to be questioned before her. On the other hand, her mother *had* to be the center of attention in any room, and here she was being told that *her* schedule was of little consequence. Percy felt her lip twitch as her mother sighed with resignation.

The waiter appeared with a couple of scarred wooden chairs. "The chief inspector asked me to rustle up some seatin'," he said. "Found these in a cupboard. There are a few more."

"Thank you," said Sir William, graciously. "If you could bring all the ones you can find. Looks like we're going to be here for some time. What is your name?"

"Syd," he replied with a toothy grin.

Sir William pressed some money into the boy's hand. "Thank you, sir."

Eventually there were enough seats for all but two of them. Bernard and Sir William opted to lean against the wall. Cecily's initial hysteria had transformed into a quiet weeping. Her mother, Agatha, had been numbed into a grief-stricken silence. The somber occasion did not invite small talk, and everyone closed their eyes as if in agitated slumber.

A sharp clap of hands shocked everyone's eyes open. "Right!" said the chief inspector. "Who's first?"

Sir William helped Cousin Agatha to her feet. The very life had drained out of her, and she looked extremely unsteady. Sir William took her arm, and they slowly followed the chief inspector down the hall. Were they going to the kitchen? The reappearance of the young waiter, who slid down the wall to sit on the floor far from them, seemed to confirm this.

Percy closed her eyes again. She tried to reconstruct what she had seen while in her tipsy fugue. She considered all the people present and immediately struck Mrs. Crabtree off the suspect list. She was not a huge fan of her mother, but the only way Mrs. Crabtree would kill anyone was by boring them to death or by accident, and this crime had been no accident. In fact, Percy couldn't countenance anyone from his own family committing the deed which left the three aristocrats. *But it couldn't be any of them.*

A reassuring thought hit her. Perhaps the murder was committed by a stranger who was committing some nefarious crime in the alley when Nigel stepped out. Wrong place, wrong time. The stranger could have struck out to eliminate a witness and fled the scene. This was a much more comfortable theory.

Someone was whistling tunelessly. Percy opened her eyes. It was the waiter, hands clasped over his bent knees.

Agatha reappeared, haggard as a soldier returning from war. Bernard's long, angular arms helped Cecily to her feet, then settled his mother-in-law into her chair. Cecily wandered back to the kitchen in a daze, handkerchief to her mouth.

Another vehicle arrived and a doctor pushed through the front door of the gallery. He hurried past them all without a comment, heading directly to the alley.

Mrs. Crabtree came to stand by Percy, who tensed. "Can you believe the effrontery of the man?"

"You mean the chief inspector?" asked Percy.

"I asked very politely if I could go first, and he completely ignored my request!"

"He gave the responsibility to Sir William, Mother. It is only right that Cousin Agatha should go first. You can see that, surely."

"I do *not!* I am a busy woman with a full schedule, and we have a city councilman coming to dinner this evening. I *have* to get back."

Here was the real reason for her mother's agitation.

"I am sure the councilman will understand once he knows the circumstances. And it's not like you are actually cooking the meal. Daddy can entertain him."

Mrs. Crabtree picked at her purple skirt. "Humphh! Your father is as useless as an ice pick in a heatwave when it comes to entertaining."

Her father's natural dynamism had leeched out, drop by drop, over forty years of hen-pecking. If he was hopeless at playing the host, it was her mother's fault.

"I doubt the councilman has high expectations of a night of revelry," Percy continued. "He and father can chat companionably over dinner and some port."

"No, no, no! That will *not* do!" cried her mother. "You don't understand. They are talking of putting a *road* at the bottom of our garden. I simply cannot allow that."

Now the truth was coming out. There was always some angle with her mother's invitations.

"I mean to persuade him that putting the road at the *other* end of the village would be a much better solution for everyone. I have maps and plans and everything."

"How careless of Nigel to spoil your scheme," said Percy, tartly.

Mrs. Crabtree jerked her head to Percy and sneered. "Watch your tone, Persephone. I am still your mother."

*Unfortunately.*

A feeble Cecily returned to the stiff embrace of her husband, and Sir William led the elderly dowager to the kitchen. While he was gone, a larger police vehicle arrived, and two more officers stepped out to retrieve a stretcher. Entering, they nodded at the assembled crowd before crunching their way to the alley.

The dowager returned relatively quickly.

"Mrs. Crabtree?" said Sir William with an artificial smile.

"About time," muttered her mother, mincing her way to the kitchen.

Though Percy had ducked into the kitchen earlier, she had not been in the frame of mind to notice any details. As she re-entered, she noticed a small window in the back wall above a large, cracked, stone sink that looked out onto the alley.

The chief inspector was seated at a table centered in the narrow room. On the tiled floor sat boxes with the word *Mystique* printed on the sides. A cabinet housed several empty bottles of champagne and two unopened ones.

"Please, sit down. Mrs. Pontefract, yes?" The attractive chief inspector was a little older than Percy. He had removed his hat to reveal glossy, chestnut waves and was now offering her a friendly smile that lit up his coppery eyes. Suddenly shy, she reached fingers up to touch her hat.

"Yes, that's me." As soon as the words were out, she regretted them. She sounded like a five-year-old.

"And your mother is—?" He consulted his notes. "Mrs. Doris Crabtree." He lifted his face with a cheeky grin. "Excuse me, *Doreece* Crabtree."

As Percy smiled back, they shared a moment. He obviously had her mother pegged, and it was a sweet victory in the middle of a bloody battle.

The ordinariness of her mother's name had been a sore trial to the woman who was scrambling up the social ladder before she could walk. If Percy had a penny for every time her mother had bemoaned the fact that Honoria had been blessed with a glorious name while she had been cursed with an utterly plebian moniker, Piers could retire. Doris was so bourgeois, Mrs. Crabtree complained. Nobility, she lamented, would never hang such a disadvantage around the neck of a beloved child. No one had the nerve to point out that Grandma and Grandfather Dungby were certainly *not* nobility.

Things had come to a head twenty years ago when, in a desperate attempt to elevate the sound of her name, Mrs. Crabtree had announced that she would now be known as *Doreece*. The pretentious news had been received to a symphony of eye rolling.

"According to my mother, she was born into the wrong family tree, Chief Inspector. She remains convinced that the heavens made an error and that she was intended for the blue bloodlines of royalty. '*Delusions of grandeur*' is the technical term, I believe."

The chief inspector pursed his lips and nodded.

"Now, what can you tell me? Why were you here today?"

She explained her relationship to Nigel.

"Were you close?" he asked, tilting his head to the side slightly. Percy had to suppress the inappropriate urge to snicker again. Perhaps it was the champagne.

"Before today, not really. We hadn't seen each other for years. The last time we were together was at my wedding, twelve years ago, and it's not like the bride can really visit with anyone. Before that, in our teens, he would tease me, so I gave him a wide berth. I'm only here today at my mother's insistence." She was babbling. *Slow down.*

"But we chatted today, and he seemed to have matured into a very nice person. Someone I could see spending more time with in the future." A large knot suddenly twisted itself around her vocal cords, and she wiped her eye with her handkerchief.

"Where were you when the body was discovered?" His pencil was poised over the page.

"I was overcome with drowsiness actually and had found one of the few chairs. I'm not used to drinking champagne in the afternoon, and it was taking effect."

"You were asleep?" His brows rose.

"Cripes, no!" she said too quickly. "Just drowsy and relaxed." Was that entirely true? Had there been some

39

minutes where she had dropped off completely? "Then Cecily screamed like a hyena and roused me better than any alarm clock. But I *was* aware, as I drifted, that not everyone was in the room. Cecily obviously, but it seemed like there were others missing. The gallery was not as full as it had been."

The chief inspector stopped writing. "But you have no recollection who was absent?"

"Not at present, but if it comes back to me, I'll let you know."

He flipped back some pages, checking his notes. "What can you tell me about the other people in attendance?"

"Well, half of them are my relatives. The other half I had not met until today." She listed the guests who were family.

"What do you think of the paintings?" asked the chief inspector, catching her off guard.

She bit the inside of her cheek. Should she disclose what Nigel had told her in confidence? He was dead so it was probably alright. "To be quite frank, this modern look is not my style, Chief Inspector. I am more of a traditionalist—" She paused, and they locked eyes. "As was my cousin."

"Care to explain?" He laced his fingers under a strong chin.

Percy related what Nigel had told her about needing to paint what was on trend to make ends meet. "One might say he had his tongue firmly planted in his cheek as he painted."

"Discovering such a thing about the artist might make someone who truly liked it angry," suggested Thompson.

"You mean, like someone who had fronted money for the exhibition?" she responded, thinking of Sir William.

"Your words not mine, Mrs. Pontefract." He moved his fingers to form a bridge. "Did Mr. Fotherington seem to have any trouble with anyone before he was found in the alley?"

An image of Nigel's intense conversation with Sir William came to mind and she mentioned it. The chief inspector dutifully recorded it in his notebook.

"I can't think of anything else," she said. "The whole event was going rather swimmingly."

"Do you have any questions for me?" he asked, unexpectedly.

Her eyes popped. "Can I ask anything?"

"Within reason. If you overstep, I'll let you know." His features melted into a magazine cover smile.

"W-what was my c-cousin st—killed with?" She almost gave herself away under his hypnotic charisma.

"A knife from this very kitchen."

This news was like a punch to her gut. Not a random act by a crazed stranger, then. Fear began an icy trail down her spine. "How can you be sure?"

"There's a knife block over there." He pointed. "And it is missing a meat knife. The one we found in your cousin is a match for the set."

Percy turned sharply in her seat, snagging the skirt of her new dress on a rough edge in the process. A gap in the block confirmed his conclusion. "Oh," was all she could manage.

She twisted the handkerchief in her hand. "I was also wondering about the nobility here. Sir William owns the gallery and fronted the money for the exhibition, but how are the others connected with Nigel?"

"A friend suggested Mr. Fotherington to Sir William." The chief inspector scanned his notes. "Lord Banbury is a modern art enthusiast and a friend of Sir William. He claims to be no authority on the subject but relies on the expertise of others. His hobby is collecting first editions. He was invited to lend a stamp of approval, I'm told. I don't believe he knew your cousin personally." Running the end of his pencil down the pages he stopped. "The dowager. Now she's a bit of a mystery. Apparently, the invitation was addressed to her son, the current earl, but he had a conflict. The dowager announced that she would represent the family."

"She didn't like the style either," said Percy. "She told Nigel to his face, and he shared his secret with her too."

"The mystery deepens," said Thompson, wiggling his eyebrows.

"It could just be eccentricity born of boredom," Percy suggested. "A trip to London might have offered a bit of excitement."

Putting a hand to her hair she realized her slouch hat had fallen back again. She must look a fright. She yanked it back in place and clutched her handbag for courage.

A sharp knock on the door made her jump.

"Enter!" barked the chief inspector, suddenly all business.

A constable entered and whispered something in his ear. Though she tried straining, she could only hear the swishing of air between his teeth.

"You are free to go, Mrs. Pontefract," said Chief Inspector Thompson. "The doctor has found a clue."

# Chapter 6

*A clue?*

Percy's curiosity quivered like a dinner gong. Could she find out what the clue was by hiding behind the door again? She was going to give it her best try.

The inspector had left in such a hurry that his pencil was still on the table. As she tried to creep to the door, her extra-large feet knocked a low shelf which rattled the pans it held.

She froze.

After several moments she decided that no one had heard and continued her less-than-graceful glide across the floor to the hallway. Looking both ways along the corridor and seeing no one, she sidled up to the back door, the only thing that separated her from the mumbled conversation on the other side. *Blast!* It was closed. She pulled it gently with her index finger, and to her delight it opened a crack. Putting her eye to the gap, she saw a slice of the chief inspector and the doctor, crouching by the body that had been turned on its side.

She gulped. Nigel's waxy face only vaguely resembled the active person he had recently been. Thankfully, his eyes were closed. She shut hers tight.

"Looks like a jade wax sealer," she heard the doctor say. "The killer must have dropped it when he thrust in the knife."

Percy put a fist to her teeth to silence a scream.

"What does the note say?" asked the inspector.

"*Outside. Back alley. 3.* It was in his inside jacket pocket. I'm surprised the murderer didn't check for it, but maybe he was interrupted. It's printed in caps, so I doubt it will be of any use."

"Or, he was worried he *might* be interrupted," weighed in the inspector. "The waiter was within earshot. If the victim made a noise or the murderer took too long, he risked being seen by the young lad. The dustbins are right here."

She heard the lid of a metal bin being lifted and the rustle of items being moved around. "What's this?"

She nervously opened one eye. Thankfully, Nigel's body had been rolled back, and all she could see was his side and the big boots of the men ready to put him on the stretcher. Did that mean the inspector and the policeman were right outside the kitchen window? She hustled back into the untidy room, her back to the wall next to the window, sliding her eyes so far to the side that they ached.

The inspector was holding something, but the doctor was blocking her view.

"There's blood on it," stated the chief inspector.

"I can't be sure until I study the body, but it looks like a match for the gash on his head."

*Nigel's head was smashed?*

"Officer, find me a specimen bag."

Percy panicked. Were the bags in the kitchen? Next to her was a small door that she hoped housed some kind of larder. She jerked open the handle to find a narrow china cupboard. Pushing her back into the shelves until it hurt, she heard the china clink. China? Her frenzied mind was firing wildly. Wasn't jade from China? Had someone mentioned a trip there? She turned her feet to the side and pulled the door to with her fingers, as far as it would go, just as she heard the crunch of big boots disappear down the hallway.

*Phew!*

She opened the cupboard door, coming face to face with the chief inspector whose even brows rose into his hairline. All his boyish charm evaporated in an instant.

"Mrs. Pontefract! What were you doing in that cupboard?"

Feeling the color drain from her face like water from a wet jumper, she looked at her feet. She needed to lie, and she was terrible at it.

"I-I fancied some more h-hors d'oeuvres. I haven't h-had caviar in ages and…"

The inspector's skeptical frown took the wind out of her sails.

"Not very appropriate when my poor cousin is laying not four feet from me." She raised sheepish eyes to the ceiling. "My stomach gets me into many scrapes." She was rambling again.

Mercifully, she was put out of her misery when the door opened to reveal the constable with a large, brown evidence bag. In her mortification she had failed to notice that the inspector was still holding something until he took the bag and placed a small, lead doorstop into it. Handing the bag to the uniformed policeman, he swept an arm toward the kitchen door.

"After you."

It was the final nail in the coffin of her humiliation.

"A doorstop?" said Mrs. Appleby when Percy told her the whole sordid story that night. "What a strange weapon."

She and Percy were sitting in the warm kitchen with three-quarters of a large Victoria sponge cake between them.

"Not really. It was probably the first thing to hand. But that's not the most extraordinary thing. What about the knife? Why did they need a *second* weapon?"

"You make a good point, Mrs. Pontefract. It does seem odd that the killer armed themselves with a doorstop if they already had a knife." In order to think better, Percy poured more double cream onto the sponge.

"Remember they had lured your cousin outside with the note," Mrs. Appleby reminded her.

"But how do we know they planned to kill him? The note just said to meet outside. It wasn't threatening. It didn't say '*or else*' or anything of that nature. Perhaps it was an innocent enough meeting that turned deadly."

"Did no one hear anything?" asked Mrs. Appleby, tucking into her own slice of cake.

"No! We were all totally aghast."

Percy had already confessed to being discovered eavesdropping in the cupboard. Mrs. Appleby had laughed so hard she had to sit down.

"Mother was her usual self." Percy pointed her spoon at the cook. "Can you believe she had the temerity to insist the chief inspector question her before the dowager?"

"What did she think of your dress?"

"She made some snide remark about it not being my color," responded Percy.

"And how did she react to the style of art?"

"Now, that was a humorous highlight. She couldn't announce her hatred of it because there were aristocrats present who were singing its praises, but I could tell she was revolted by it and she called Picasso 'Paulo Peaches'. It was hilarious!"

They dissolved into laughter again.

"And you say they are going to put a main road right behind your father's land?" Mrs. Appleby wiped her eyes with the bottom of her apron.

"Can you imagine? My poor father must have to listen to her complain about it every single day. That city councilman will wish he'd never been born by the time she's finished with him."

Mrs. Appleby tipped her head and twisted her mouth. "Progress," she said. "Can't really stop it, can you?"

"Well, my mother will do her darndest."

As Percy scraped the pattern off her plate, Mrs. Appleby asked, "So do you have any theories about who murdered Nigel?"

"Not yet. I need to follow up on some things. I think someone mentioned going to China. It wasn't to me, but I overheard a snippet of the conversation. It was while I was drowsy. I need to find out who that was, because it could be a link to the jade stamp."

Mrs. Appleby got up and rummaged through the junk drawer finally handing Percy her notepad and a pencil.

She opened the cover and immediately saw her notes for the murder at the Christmas party which brought back a flood of guilt that her friend Phoebe was now in Holloway women's prison.

"Oh, no you don't!" cried Mrs. Appleby as Percy hesitated over the page, her mouth pulling down. "Mrs. Valentine got no more than she deserved. It was not your fault she committed treason and was an accomplice to murder."

Percy looked up with haunted eyes.

"And who knows how many servicemen's lives you saved by uncovering their treason?"

"It doesn't feel like much of a victory," Percy murmured.

"Fresh page, love," said Mrs. Appleby tapping the table next to the notebook.

Percy did as she was bid and picked up the pencil. "Right. Item number one. *Has anyone recently traveled to China?* I can bring it up in conversation at the funeral." She wrote slowly with beautiful penmanship. She had suffered from the inability to read her scribbling in the last case. *"Second, who was missing right before Cecily screamed?"* She chewed the pencil. *"Why did Sir William Packett finance the exhibition, and is Lord Banbury really a lover of Cubist art?"* She pushed her tight curls behind her ear. "Honestly, I can't see how anyone is. And lastly, *why did*

*the dowager travel all the way to London for the gallery
event when it was her son who received the invitation?* I
suggested to the inspector that she might have viewed it as
a bit of an adventure, but I don't really believe that."

The phone rang in the hall.

"I'll get it," said Percy, stealing a bite from the cake in
the middle of the table before she left.

The hall felt chilly after the warmth of the kitchen with
its cozy Aga. She sat in the little chair beside the telephone
table and picked up the cold receiver.

"Fetching 548."

"Persephone." *Mother.* "Prepare yourself! I have terrible
news."

# Chapter 7

Percy's heart beat a little faster. "Has someone been arrested?"

"Arrested? Good heavens, girl what are you talking about?" snapped her mother.

"For Nigel's murder."

An exclamation of frustration made its way down the line. "This is much more important than that. Your father did *not* talk to the councilman about the road business, and he had left before I could present my case."

Percy's eyes hit the tops of their orbit. "Mother! How can you blather on about the road when Agatha's son has had his head bashed in?"

"Head? I thought he was stabbed in the chest?"

*Oops!*

"Yes, of course. Silly me. Don't you think you are being a little insensitive?"

"Nonsense! I can't bring him back, Persephone. Life must go on, and I need to stop that road."

Percy began to wind a lock of wiry hair around her finger as she let her mother's whinging become background noise, punctuating her flow with the odd 'hmm' or 'oh' until her mother's arguments were all exhausted.

"Will you be going to the funeral?" Percy asked.

"Of course. They are family. It is my—our duty. I have told your father he must put in an appearance."

"I shall have to see if my black dress still fits. I seem to have put on weight since Christmas."

"I am glad you brought that up, Persephone. Though I do not agree with the current trend for pencil thin bodies, I *am* of the school of thought that a woman should watch her weight for her husband's sake."

Percy blinked. "Excuse me?"

"Piers married a woman who was, if not slender, not overweight. It's not fair to him if you turn into something he didn't bargain for."

The nerve of the woman! "Mother! Piers loves me for who I am." She screwed up her courage. "And people in glass houses really shouldn't throw stones."

"That is a false argument. It is natural for women of a certain age to spread. I might even go so far as to say it is natural."

Steam was shooting out of Percy's ears. She had to end this conversation before she said something she regretted. "What is that, Mrs. Appleby? Look, Mother, I have to go. I'll see you at the funeral."

She crashed the handset into the cradle, every ounce of her smarting. Why did each conversation with Mother strip her of the little self-confidence she had?

A bundle of letters fell through the door onto the mat as Percy bounced down the stairs a few days later. One off-white envelope stood out from the brown ones containing bills. Scooping up the pile, she pulled the white one to the top and turned it over. A red wax seal stared back at her.

Pushing into the kitchen she grabbed a knife and sliced the envelope open, maintaining the seal intact, and extracting an invitation to tea with the Dowager Countess of Kent. She plopped down onto a seat in surprise.

"What's that, then?" asked Mrs. Appleby as Percy tapped the thick card on the table.

Percy showed her the invitation and then turned the envelope in her direction.

"A wax seal," Mrs. Appleby said as if she were an actress in a radio drama. Percy half-expected a sinister crash of symbols.

"We can't jump to conclusions, Mrs. A. I would wager that all aristocratic families have their own wax seal and probably many middle-class ones too."

Mrs. Appleby sucked in her cheeks. "Why do you think she wants to see you?"

"I honestly have no idea, but since she is on the list of people I want to question, I'm going to accept."

Unsurprisingly, the dowager lived in Kent, but fortunately it was in a part of the county that wasn't too far from Percy's part of Surrey.

Chiltern Park was an imposing former fortress. As Percy approached in her little green car, it was hard not to be impressed by the lake that reflected the whole structure in its surface. She pulled over to admire it. The vast edifice included a fort with two separate square battlements that had to be at least four hundred years old. After a moment of contemplation, Percy continued on, but as she got closer, she was astonished to see that the lake was not as close to the house as it had appeared from a distance, and that the part of the building she could see was actually the back of the property. As she neared, it was apparent that a more recent structure had been built onto the back of the old fortress. She drove around a large, grassy area in the front until she reached a meandering gravel driveway.

Parking her humble Ford on a great sweep of gravel, she crunched her way to the imposing front door. Though she was wearing her second-best day outfit, upon seeing the grandeur of the place, she worried about being mistaken for a servant or common vendor. She grasped the invite firmly between her finger and thumb just in case the validity of her authority to use the front door was questioned.

A man whose eyes and jaw were all headed south answered the door, droopy nose in the air as if he were a bloodhound who had smelled something offensive.

"May I help you?" His words were elongated as though they were wading their way through honey.

Percy presented her invitation.

"Ah." He opened the door wider and stepped back to allow her entry into a vestibule that was all dark wood paneling with artisan carvings and deep red walls. The whole thing was filled with muted red rugs to cover the stone floors and reduce the chance of echo. A magnificent balustrade stairway split into two, a huge painting of a nobleman and his hunting dogs at the point where the stairs divided. The balcony stretched across the top of the room on both sides like a giant minstrel's gallery. At the bottom of the stairway was a sizeable fireplace.

Percy had never entered a house so utterly magnificent, and she suddenly felt incredibly small, a condition she had not experienced since childhood.

"Follow me," proclaimed the butler after watching her drink in the general splendor.

She followed him down a wide hallway, lined with the same paneling as the entrance, bumping a pedestal table enroute and only catching an expensive vase from destruction in the nick of time. At length, he opened the door of a more intimate room decorated in every shade of blue with an abundance of comfortable velvet armchairs situated in conversation pairs around a large, roaring fireplace. The ceiling was filled with ornate plaster carvings of grapes, and a large, crystal chandelier hung in the middle of the room.

Seated in one of the chairs was the formal dowager in another gown reminiscent of a bygone era.

"Mrs. Pontefract," pronounced the butler as though she were next in line for the guillotine.

52

"I am *so* glad you could come," said the dowager in her crackly voice. "Do sit down, my dear."

The heat in the room was oppressive, and Percy wondered if she should remove her coat.

Paralyzed by indecision, the dowager saved her. "Brainsworth, take Mrs. Pontefract's fur coat."

Percy slipped out of her best fur which held only a faint scent of mothballs and handed it to the butler. Unfortunately, the removal did little to relieve her of the heat and a prickle of sweat burst through her hairline.

The old lady's face split into a crêpey smile that suspended the draping wrinkles temporarily. Percy wondered again why on earth such an aged woman as the dowager had made the journey to London for her cousin's unusual art exhibit.

"I was impressed by you in London," the dowager began. "You seem like a reasonable and intelligent woman." She pointed to a three-tiered cake stand. "Cake?"

Pushing memories of the last conversation with her mother aside, Percy reached for a dainty square covered in pastel-pink icing.

"Would you mind pouring? My wrist is giving me trouble." The dowager rubbed her arm.

After taking a bite of the decadent, fondant cream cake, Percy picked up the elaborately decorated tea pot and poured two cups.

"How is your aunt faring?" asked the dowager.

"Oh, Agatha Fotherington is not my aunt," explained Percy. "Nigel was my second cousin. His mother is my mother's first cousin."

"I see." She narrowed her steely eyes.

"My aunt *was* there as it happens—my mother's sister. Honoria Longdale, and my Uncle Frederick."

The dowager's eyes widened. "The woman in the obscenely large, green feathered hat?"

53

Percy was shaken by the dowager's straightforward style. "The very one."

The dowager chewed on this information before declaring, "Agatha Fotherington, then. How is she coping?"

"I haven't seen or spoken to her since the awful..."— Percy searched for a word that would not be too jarring in this comfortable room—"...events. I imagine she's devastated. Nigel was just emerging as an important artist. On the brink of greatness, I might even say."

"I believe she is a widow." The dowager took a sip of tea, little finger extended. "How did you find Mr. Fotherington at the exhibit?"

Percy placed her cake on the little table. "That is the saddest part. When we were younger, he was a nasty tease, but he had matured into a lovely human being. Now I have been robbed of the chance to renew my acquaintance with him."

A sleek, black cat slunk around the dowager's chair and fixed its green gaze on Percy. She tensed. She did not have a happy history with cats.

"I suppose you are attending the funeral?"

Keeping her eye on the whereabouts of the cat, Percy said, "Yes."

"Then please give his mother my deepest condolences."

"I will."

The dowager took another sip and sighed with delight as though she didn't drink tea several times a day, every day. "Are the police any further forward in their investigation?"

Was this why she had been asked to tea? "I have no idea." Should she divulge what she had overheard? "But I do believe Nigel was struck in the head before being—"

"Thrust through with a knife." The dowager's fragile smile slipped. "That is news to me. Why would someone need to kill the poor boy twice?"

"Perhaps the first blow did not succeed and the killer wanted to be sure."

The dowager nodded and ground her false teeth. "Did that police inspector seem competent to you?"

"Chief Inspector Thompson?" She thought of the charismatic chief inspector and then the shame of being discovered in the china cabinet. "I don't have too much experience with police inspectors, but he seemed adequate."

The dowager sniffed. "I hope he's more than 'adequate' to give the poor mother some closure."

Percy warred with her conscience momentarily. "I know he found some clues by the body."

The dowager's silver eyebrows rose into curlicues. "Oh?"

"It occurred while they were questioning me, and I happened to overhear a bit." This was stretching the truth like an old elastic band, but it was better than appearing to be a snoop. "They had to roll Nigel to see how far the knife had penetrated, and that's when they found the stamp."

"A postage stamp?"

"No, the kind you use to seal envelopes with wax."

The old lady glanced to the side. "How odd."

Percy, now on a roll, was doling out information like a runaway train. "That's not all. When they saw the gash on his head the inspector looked in the bin and found a lead door stop with blood on it."

"Then I would say this inspector has already proved to be more than adequate." She folded veined hands in her lap. "Perhaps you can keep me informed of his progress since I am no longer involved with the family. I should like to know the conclusion."

"If you wish," said Percy, squashing some crumbs onto her finger and popping them into her mouth when the dowager was not looking. As she reached for another delicacy, the cat stalked toward her. Putting her fears aside she grabbed a slice of treacle tart.

"I understand that your second cousin painted traditional works as well as the monstrosities on display in Chelsea."

Percy had just taken a huge bite of the treacle slice. Her eyes bulged as she tried to chew quickly in order to answer the dowager's question, but swallowing too fast, she choked and had to take a gulp of tea to free her windpipe. She wiped her eyes and dabbed at her nose before managing to wheeze, "I think so." She could have sworn the cat smirked.

"You have not seen his other works then?"

"No, but he had just promised to show them to me when..." A wave of melancholy washed over her. "He won't be able to do that now."

The dowager turned a large ring around an arthritic finger as the cat jumped onto her lap. "Now, tell me about your family."

Percy spent the next ten minutes briefing the old lady about her boys. She flattered herself that the dowager seemed genuinely interested.

Stroking the black cat's head, the dowager said, "It may surprise you to know that my father was Russian. He moved to England after he married my mother. She is a De Montfort." She swept her arm. "This house is actually *her* ancestral home. Since her father had no male heirs and the estate was not entailed, as the oldest daughter, she inherited."

Percy was not well versed in the inheritance laws ruling the upper classes, but she was pretty sure that a Russian would not assume his father in law's title in England.

"I see you are wondering how my son could be an earl. My mother only bore daughters also, and as the eldest I inherited the house. I married the Earl of Kent who was our neighbor. We were childhood sweethearts and I begged him to live here with me in my beloved childhood home. Now that he is gone, my son is the sixth earl."

"Do you speak Russian?" Percy asked.

"I do. As does my son. But we do not speak it except at home these days." She paused. "My father was a Romanov."

Percy's eyes grew wide, and the dowager grew solemn. "The family we had left behind were all killed in the revolution."

Percy was lost for words and merely stared at her empty cup.

The dowager clapped her hands. "Enough of sadness! Would you like a tour?"

# *Chapter 8*

After the funeral they all gathered at Agatha's orange brick, square Victorian house. Set in three acres of woodlands, the structure was pleasantly symmetrical with two bay windows flanking the front door and an additional two windows on the far side of each, and five windows on the upper floor bordered with white wood.

The narrow entry was divided by the stairs, and a hallway led to a kitchen in the back which had originally been a separate building, well before Nigel's family had bought the property. The Fotheringtons had a cook and a maid, who led them all to the front drawing room.

Agatha had the look of someone emerging from a terrible nightmare, and Percy realized that as a widow, Nigel's mother had probably leaned on her only son a great deal.

Cecily looked done in, too. Percy did not know if the two Fotherington children had been close, but regardless, losing one's only brother to murder was traumatic. Her angular husband sat on the arm of the chair she occupied, his arm limply around her shoulders. Dressed in black, his bony frame appeared even more gaunt, if that were possible.

Percy's father had come under duress; not because he did not care for his wife's cousin but because it meant he was forced to spend a whole day in the company of his wife, unable to steal away to his beloved garden or the local pub. However, he did successfully install himself alone in a forgotten alcove with a plate full of goodies.

Piers had not come because Nigel was not a direct relative and because he tried to avoid Percy's mother the same way her father did.

Percy had needed assistance with the zip on her black mourning dress. Thankfully the fabric had some give.

Perusing the nibbles she decided on three sausage rolls, two cucumber sandwiches and a generous slice of chocolate cake. She found a vacant chair and balanced the plate on her knee before realizing she had forgotten to get herself a drink.

Her aunt and uncle were on the other side of the room tucking into one of everything as her mother regaled them about the projected road. If Percy moved to get some punch it would put her directly in her mother's path. She decided not to venture and instead, wait for the maid to reappear.

The room was quite full. There was a whole group of people she had never met, and Percy felt perfectly at liberty to stay on the fringes people-watching. Surprisingly, there were several stylish women in attendance. One woman in particular caught her eye—a pretty brunette with a chignon and a tragic mien. None of them had been at the exhibition. It would appear that Nigel was a confirmed bachelor. There were a couple of artist types, their dark clothes hanging from sparse frames, eyes full of angst. She briefly wondered if that was due to the occasion or their chosen occupation.

Older couples she assumed to be neighbors from the village, made up the rest of the group, chatting with the ease of familiarity.

As Percy finished her third sausage roll, her mother approached. She stiffened.

"It still fits, I see," she sneered, referring to Percy's dress. She clicked her tongue. "No one appreciates the gravity of the proposed road like I do. Honoria merely smiled, offering no sympathy."

Doris and her sister had been in competition since the day her sibling was born. The only benefit of Honoria's arranged marriage was that her husband had better prospects than Percy's father. As the older sister by three years, Doris had owned a home first, but as soon as Honoria married, they were gifted a large country house with its own stables. Horrified at being upstaged, Percy's mother had immediately put her home up for sale and bought one larger and on more land than Honoria's, in spite of not really being able to afford it. But her father was a bank manager and as such could approve his own loan. The property was nicely situated on the edge of a village that boasted two stately homes within four miles. Her mother would rather die than move out of the sphere of their influence.

Mrs. Crabtree had wielded the production of children as a battering ram for years, but Honoria never buckled. She merely gloated about the exotic holidays she and her husband enjoyed with the money they saved on school fees. This ongoing feud meant Aunt Honoria had zero sympathy for her social climbing sister's plight.

Percy searched desperately for a means of escape; once her mother began a tirade, she was not eager to stop.

"Silly me, I forgot a drink. Have my seat, Mother. I'm parched."

Before her mother could object, Percy jumped up and bolted to the drinks table, grabbing a few more sandwiches and sidling up to her aunt and uncle.

"Nice service," said Uncle Frederick in an insincere monotone, his words merely filling the silence between them.

The funeral had actually been rather impersonal since the vicar was newish and did not know Nigel, but it was the kind of thing one felt obliged to say.

"Mmm," Percy murmured non-committally. "How are you feeling about the whole thing, Aunt Honoria? You were near the murder when it happened weren't you?"

"What makes you say that?" Her aunt's lazy face pulled tight with indignation.

"Oh, I just meant that I didn't see the pair of you in the gallery right before Cecily came in and there weren't many places to go, so I just assumed."

"We were there," Honoria retorted. "We must have been on the other side of the room where you couldn't see us."

Percy was almost certain they had *not* been in the room, so why the need to lie? She wished she could remember who else had been absent.

"Have you seen any of Nigel's other stuff?" she asked. "His less avant-garde works?"

"I didn't know there were any. Thank heavens!" Honoria dropped her voice. "I've been embarrassed to think those odd paintings might tarnish our family name."

Percy felt a bark of laughter germinate from deep down within and stuffed a sandwich into her mouth to prevent its escape. Once her voice box was under control she ventured, "Nigel was going to show them to me. I wonder if Agatha could let me have a look."

"How much longer do we have to stay?" moaned her uncle, flattening the thin, oiled strands on his pate for the thousandth time.

"Not until at least half the people have left, Frederick. It would be a huge social faux pas if we left before the locals and might lead to ugly gossip."

Tired of the self-centeredness of her relatives, Percy glided across the room to Agatha's side. "How *are* you?"

"Lovely service, don't you think?" Agatha parroted. "Reminds me of his father's funeral." A sob broke through and Percy let her grieve for a moment.

"Nigel mentioned that he also paints in a more traditional style. He was going to show me. I don't suppose you would let me take a peek?"

Through watery eyes her mother's cousin peered at her. "Oh, they aren't here. He lived in a garret apartment in Dexford which had space for him to keep a studio." The lines on her forehead gathered together. "I could give you a key, if you are really interested."

The idea that Percy could search his flat without witnesses was as satisfying as scratching an elusive itch.

61

"Are you sure?" Percy responded. "I wouldn't like to invade his privacy." Though in truth that was exactly what she wanted to do.

"No. Nigel would want you to, Percy. I'll get you a key. The police have already desecrated the place, so to speak. I can't face going over there to clean it out just yet. Perhaps you could give it an airing?"

When Agatha had given her the key and address, Percy decided it was time to speak to Nigel's sister, Cecily. In the ten days since the murder, she had lost a significant amount of weight making her jaw poke angrily through the skin and her eyes to appear larger than they really were.

"Cecily." She kissed her cheek, the skin clammy against her own. "Bernard." She nodded at him.

"Wasn't it dreadful?" Cecily cried, a touch of loathing in her tone. "The vicar said things that weren't accurate. I had to stop myself standing up in the middle of it all and screaming." This was the first honest comment about the dreary service.

Bernard patted his wife's arm. "Nigel hadn't lived here in years, darling. How could you expect the poor vicar to know your brother?"

"He should have been buried where he lived," she muttered.

"Did he go to church in Dexford?" Bernard asked.

Cecily blew air out of her nose with contempt. "I hardly think so."

"Then isn't it better that the service be held in a place he used to call home, where people know his family?"

"I suppose so," she agreed, grudgingly.

"Have the police made any progress in the investigation?" Percy asked.

"Oh, Percy you don't know! They told us Nigel was hit on the head and *then* stabbed. Why the need to hurt the dear boy twice?" Cecily started to shake and took out a well-

62

used handkerchief. Bernard guided Percy away from his wife.

"They did inform us they do not believe it was a random thug in the alley. They questioned the other shop owners and they saw no one. But more importantly, the knife was from the gallery kitchen and Nigel had a note in his pocket to meet someone in the alley."

It took all of Percy's willpower to refrain from saying 'I know'. However, the revelation that none of the other shop owners had seen a stranger loitering in the alley was news.

"So, it was one of us." Percy felt the chill of unease in her bones.

"Looks like it." Bernard agreed.

"Have you done much criminal law?" Percy asked him.

"Not a lot. Mostly tax evasion and libel. But I did dip my toe in last year. We defended the baronet accused of stealing a diamond watch in Hatton Garden. We got him off. Perhaps you heard about it?"

"No," Percy replied. "Was he innocent?"

Bernard pinched his lips. "Our policy is not to ask. We presented the case as a misunderstanding. My senior counsel used quite a few of my suggestions for closing arguments." Bernard almost grabbed his jacket lapels with pride but flicked a nonexistent speck of dust from them instead.

"Do the police have any suspects?" she asked.

"Well, they have to tread carefully. It was not their usual lineup. They would have to have ironclad evidence before carting a peer off to jail." His laugh was staccato, like a coughing donkey. When he saw that she was not laughing he cleared his throat. "No. Not that they have told us. That's why dear Cecily is so burdened. She cannot sleep with her brother's killer still on the loose."

He hadn't mentioned the jade stamp. Should she bring it up?

"There were no other clues?"

63

Bernard screwed up his aphid-like face in thought. "I don't think so."

Looking back at his wife who was weeping again, he said, "I should get back to Cecily."

"Of course. And it is time for me to go. I have a long journey ahead of me." She scanned the room for her mother. She would be obliged to say goodbye.

Mrs. Crabtree had cornered her brother-in-law again. His expression bore the unmistakable melancholy of a man pleading for intercession.

Hoping to make a quick getaway, Percy strode over, spinning on her heel. "I'm off."

Before she was out of her mother's circle of reach, a claw-like hand grabbed her sleeve.

*Bother!*

"I was just telling Frederick about the obnoxious plans for the new road. He agrees that it is the wrong place to put a thoroughfare and will cause traffic jams."

Percy looked at her uncle whose eyes pled with her to kill him quickly. Instead, still in her mother's clutches, she gave him a quick side hug.

"I'll see you to the door," he begged, with no small amount of desperation.

"No need," she assured him.

He held up a hand to stop her. "Nonsense. Manners and all that." She saw a tic jiggle the lid of his left eye.

She should not toy with the man. "If you insist."

In the front entrance, he held up Percy's coat. She slipped her arms in. "Your mother is like a dog with a bone when she is passionate about something. Never lets it go!"

"That is a wickedly accurate description, Uncle Frederick. I'm sorry you had to put up with all that."

"It's your father I feel sorry for," he said with feeling.

"Daddy! I quite forgot he was here. Where is he? I should say goodbye."

Her uncle dabbed his forehead with the back of his hand. "Percy, have a heart. If you try to find your father, it will only bring him to the attention of your mother. Take pity on him and just leave. The poor man has to make the drive home with her, as it is."

It was a good point. "Can you tell him goodbye from me, Uncle Frederick?"

"Will do!" He pulled a handkerchief from his pocket, and something went flying. Percy bent over to pick it up.

It was a cube of red wax.

# Chapter 9

The hearty smell of bacon drew Percy to the kitchen like the Pied Piper's flute.

"Morning!" said Mrs. Appleby. "Sit yourself down and I'll get your plate ready."

Percy had spent a restless night, dropping into light naps where nightmares of her uncle smashing Nigel in the head with red cubes of wax haunted her.

Mrs. Appleby busied herself at the Aga. "You got in late."

"It is quite far away," said Percy with a yawn.

"How was it?" Mrs. Appleby presented her with a steaming full English and Percy's mouth began to water.

"Pretty impersonal if you must know. The vicar didn't know Nigel well, so all his heartiness was a bit forced."

"Were there many people?" The cook pulled out a chair and returned to her own breakfast.

"It is not a large church, but it was full. Nigel grew up there and many of the other villagers are long-time friends of the family." Percy shook the salt and pepper over her plate and breathed in the delightful scent.

"That's nice. How was your mother?" Mrs. Appleby was well aware of the quirks of Mrs. Crabtree.

Percy huffed. "Her usual self but it was worse because we were at the funeral of a family member where it was dreadfully inappropriate to harp on about the proposed road." She slipped in a bite of bacon dripping with egg yolk. "I hardly spoke to Father who was hiding himself away from Mother. At home he has developed quite a clever schedule. He takes the dogs for long walks early in the morning, checks his garden up until lunch time. Then he goes to the library to work on his 'History of Elmtree'. After supper he wanders off to the local pub and stays until closing. Mother is already asleep by then. But yesterday he

66

couldn't avoid her, poor dear. I expect he will need all day to recover."

Mrs. Appleby chuckled as she rubbed Apollo's head and slipped him a piece of bacon which Percy pretended not to notice.

"Agatha looked shell shocked. The exhibition was supposed to be Nigel's moment of glory. She must feel very alone. I know she has Cecily, but still." Percy loaded her fork with grilled tomato and fried egg.

"Do the family know any more about the murder?" the cook asked, both hands around a mug of tea.

"Not really. But they did tell me the police have confirmed that it was not a stranger because the knife used was from the kitchen. Gave me the wobblies, actually. Oh, and Cecily and Bernard did not mention the jade stamp. I don't know if it was an oversight or if the police haven't told them."

Percy cut into the second fried egg so that the rich, yellow yolk dribbled out and onto the crispy toast. "There was one thing," she said, putting another bite into her mouth and swooning. "When I was saying goodbye to Uncle Frederick, a red wax cube flew out of his pocket when he reached for his hankie."

Mrs. Appleby's cup stopped midway to her mouth. "Could be a coincidence."

"Are you really suggesting that Uncle Frederick killed Nigel?" asked Percy indignantly.

"Are you?" Mrs. Appleby looked like a curious badger.

"Of course not!" declared Percy, holding her fork like a trident.

"Why did you mention it then?" Mrs. Appleby's gray eyebrow was cocked like a gun.

Percy relaxed her grip on the fork. "Oh, alright! I suppose I was in a way. But there is no circumstance under which Uncle Frederick would murder anyone, let alone a family member."

Mrs. Appleby pushed up from the table and went to the dresser to retrieve Percy's notebook.

Percy frowned. "What's this for?"

"You should write down what you learned yesterday."

"I just told you; I didn't really learn anything." She popped a juicy piece of fried bread into her mouth.

"That's not entirely true. You told me the family doesn't know about the jade stamp," contradicted Mrs. Appleby.

Percy sighed and grabbed the pencil. "I'll give you that."

"And you should at least put down that your uncle has wax for a stamp."

"Alright." She began to scribble then remembered her resolution to write more clearly.

"I'll bet there were other subtle things you noticed that were not spoken."

Percy scratched her head. "There were several beautiful women there, which I found odd since Nigel didn't have a special someone in his life. If he had, she would have been at the exhibit."

Mrs. Appleby smiled widely exposing her crooked teeth. "See, you're becoming a real detective."

The food was beginning to nourish Percy's brain. "And skinny little Cecily had lost more weight. She looked like a puff of wind would knock her over. Perhaps she and Nigel were closer than I thought." She scraped the last of the yolk from her plate onto the final bite of bacon on her fork. "Oh, and Nigel lived in Hampshire. A place called Dexford, in a garret flat which he used as a studio. Agatha gave me the key so I could look at his other work."

"There you go then. Another lead." The cook took her plate and cup and put them in the sink to wash.

"The police will have already searched his home," Percy pointed out.

"You have more faith in their thoroughness than I do," said Mrs. Appleby with a wink. "I'll bet they missed something."

Dexford was a middle sized, dormitory town in the heart of Hampshire. Percy had taken a first-class train to Bideford-upon-Avon and then a taxi. Nigel's flat was above a high-end shoe shop called *Porter's* in the pretty, Elizabethan high street.

She entered the shop and a thin, attractive young woman approached, her hands clasped by her waist.

"How can I help you today, madam?"

"Oh, I'm not here for shoes," Percy explained. "I am a cousin of the tenant of the flat upstairs. I have permission to look through his paintings."

The shopgirl's expression descended into what could only be called, 'gossip face'. "The nice man who was killed?"

"Yes. I want to buy one of his paintings as a memento."

"Do they know why someone would—" she looked over her shoulder and asked sotto voce—"murder him?"

"Not yet," replied Percy.

"He was always nice to me," the pretty girl said, flashing her eyes, "and he would even—"

A sharp throat clearing caused them both to whip around. A short, bald man was pinching his lips and blinking rapidly behind heavy black frames.

The girl stepped away from Percy. "Oh, Mr. Porter. This lady is cousin to Mr. Fotherington."

The owner turned his fluttering eyes to Percy.

"I just wanted to alert you that I will be in the flat above in case you thought it was an intruder."

The little man pulled at a gold chain that hung from his tweed waistcoat and checked the time. "I assume you have some form of identification?"

"Ah, I-uh." Percy's lips pulled into a shrug. Then enlightenment dawned. "I have a key."

His demeanor softened. "Splendid." He rested his hands on his belly. "I appreciate you warning us. Terrible business. I wonder, do you know if the family will be removing his belongings any time soon?"

"Cousin Agatha, his mother, did not mention anything to me, but I can give you her phone number."

He swung an arm toward the counter. "That would be most convenient."

Percy wrote down the number on a pad next to the till.

"I hope you find what you are looking for," he tweeted as she left.

A narrow alley to the left of the building revealed another door. She fitted the key in the lock, and it turned easily. Pushing the door, she felt resistance; it was stuck on a pile of letters. She gave it a shove. The door opened onto a very small square of linoleum that led to a steep staircase. Picking up the mail, Percy closed the door and locked it securely behind her. Visiting the home of a dead man was giving her the creeps.

At the top of the stairs was an airy, garret apartment that ran the whole width of the shop below. The flat was one, grand, vaulted room with large windows through which the sun was pouring. Perfect light for an artist. Space on one side was filled with easels and unfinished canvases, tubes of paint and brushes everywhere. *Chaos.* On the other was huddled a single, messy bed, a small table and one chair, a sizeable oven and a tiny sink. The bathroom must have been outside in the back yard.

She placed the pile of mail on the table and took off her coat, hanging it on the back of the chair. Large drop cloths lay on the floor like abandoned burial shrouds.

Stepping carefully, Percy examined the first easel. It held an unfinished portrait. She recognized one of the stylish women from the funeral—the mournful beauty with the jet-black hair. Nigel had captured her in the middle of an amusing thought. It was good. Very good.

70

The second easel held one of the uncomfortable, modern pieces, but only the harsh, black lines had thus far been painted. The rest was merely sketch.

Wandering further she came face to face with a large seascape during a summer storm. Waves curled and fringed with white foam, surrounded a colorful lighthouse out on a small island. It was so evocative she could almost taste the salt.

Moving to the back of the room, she saw rows of canvases standing upright, leaning against the wall. She began to flick through them. In the first stack were several more portraits and running, wild horses, every detail of their muscles rippling under shiny coats. Further back, her heart caught as she stared at a smaller version of the seascape. She wondered if her aunt would sell it to her. This painting would be perfect for the space above the bed in her room and would be a magnificent keepsake of her cousin. She slid it out and placed it in the front of the stack.

Moving to the next pile she discovered more of the obnoxious modern stuff and was tempted to abandon the job when her fingers pulled forward a canvas that revealed a picture that stopped her dead in her tracks. Staring back at her was the *Girl with a Pearl Earring* by Vermeer.

Why was a copy of the famous picture among Nigel's work? Were there others? She quickly flicked through all the piles but came up empty. She placed the Vermeer replica at the front of the pile and went to sit on the spindly chair to reflect.

Sitting next to the smaller version of the seascape, she could tell that the Vermeer was different. It appeared to be very old. But how could that be? Was it legal to make reproductions of old masters? So many questions. She would need to consult an art historian.

She retrieved the imitation Vermeer and took it toward the window wall. In the light, fine cracks in the oil paint were evident. Was she, in fact, holding the original? Was Nigel an art thief?

Replacing the picture at the back of the pile, she decided to conduct a thorough search of the entire flat. Dropping onto her knees, she peered under the simple iron bed using her hands. As she swept them back and forth, they made contact with a sharp object. Grasping it between her fingers, she extracted a tiny, diamond butterfly brooch. After examining it for some time, she wrapped it in a clean handkerchief and dropped it into her voluminous handbag.

Rubbing the dust from her hands she moved over to the bin. It was half full, and she remembered the inspector poking around in the dustbins with a pencil after the murder. She found such an item in her handbag and jabbed it into the pile of rubbish, past old fish and chip wrappers, waxed sandwich paper and potato peels. Near the bottom she found a crumpled paper. Closing her eyes and holding her nose, she pushed her hand into the bottom of the bin and withdrew the smelly, stained note.

Taking it to the table, she spread out the sheet, flattening the folds.

It was a receipt. *For £1000!* She smoothed the paper again. It was handwritten to Nigel but was not a formal receipt that one might receive from a jeweler. It did not even list the item sold except with a number. The ink had faded from wet items placed on top of it in the bin and she took it over to the window.

*147.*

Folding it carefully, she placed the receipt into her handbag with the brooch and went back to the Vermeer. Withdrawing it for the second time, she turned the canvas over. In pencil on the wooden frame was written the number *148*. Her heart sank.

Nigel was painting forgeries.

# Chapter 10

The acrid smell of old wood and furniture polish made Percy wrinkle her nose as she sat in the waiting room of Mr. Grace, the Surrey art expert's office. A spring from the chair was pinching her in a most distressing fashion as she clutched the large paper bag containing possible contraband to her chest. The white head of the elderly secretary was bent over the most untidy scrawl Percy had ever seen. She shifted to find a more comfortable position but instead found another errant spring.

"Mrs…" A thin man in spectacles was peering at a piece of paper held between his long fingers. "…Pontefract?" His wrinkled brow formed an 'n' as he shifted the glasses up his expansive forehead.

Percy stood, pulling down her dress before following his spare frame down a dark, paneled hallway. Entering a surprisingly large office, her shoe caught the edge of a sturdy Turkish rug, pitching her forward until she stopped her forward momentum by grabbing hold of the back of a deep, leather chair. She breathed thanks that the art expert was turned the other way as she tightened her grip on the painting and checked the position of her hat. Large, leaded windows on either side of an antique marble fireplace added a sense of gravity and solemnity to the room, and old country landscapes hung around the space.

Mr. Grace Esq. made a pyramid with those long fingers. "I understand you want me to look at a piece of art."

"Yes," she replied, reaching into the bag and pulling out the Vermeer replica.

The serious man pulled back in shock, even as he reached forward for the painting. Percy had chosen not to warn him of the content of the picture in advance, deciding instead to say she had found the painting in the attic of a deceased relative and wanted it valued.

His lithe fingers twitched as he placed the picture reverently on his desk and removed the wire spectacles to pick up a small magnifying glass that he fixed into his eye like a monocle. Hands fanned out, moving slowly over the top of the painting, he stopped at intervals murmuring to himself. This continued for almost half an hour.

He finally removed the small glass, which left a red ring around his wrinkled eye, and replaced his glasses.

"Do you recognize this painting, Mrs. Pontefract?" he asked, head inclined like a knowledgeable college professor.

"Well, of course. I saw it hanging in the National Gallery many years ago," she responded.

He pointed to the canvas with a wry smile. "Not this exact one, obviously."

"Naturally," she replied, while inwardly breathing a sigh of relief that she wasn't handling stolen property. "But I did want your opinion on the quality."

He drummed his curious fingers on the desk. "The original was loaned to the National Gallery for a period of five years and was then sent back to the owner and displayed privately in an undisclosed location, where I understand it still resides." He looked up squeezing one eye almost closed. "If I did not already know that I would be inclined to think the original was sitting on my desk at this very moment."

"So, it's good then?" Her heart raced.

"It is *more* than good," stated Mr. Grace. "In fact, it is the best forgery I have ever seen." Tipping his head, chin resting on clasped hands, he said, "May I ask where you really got this?"

An annoying pulse began to beat in her temple. "I am not at liberty to say, but I can tell you I am going straight to the police when I leave here. I wanted to make sure of its quality before approaching them with my suspicions."

74

"The oils have been put through an aging process that render it almost impossible to detect as a forgery. It is exquisite." He leaned back, elbows on the arms of his chair. "Let me posit a theory to you, Mrs. Pontefract."

Percy's hands gripped the handles of her handbag, beads of sweat popping out across her upper lip.

"I conjecture that this forgery was painted with the intent that it be passed off on the black market as the original, in a private sale, to an unsuspecting buyer."

Percy gulped. "I have no idea. Like I said, I found it."

"My main concern is that if the artist has created other fakes of this quality that have already been sold to collectors by unscrupulous agents, it could undermine the integrity of the art collection industry as a whole." He brushed at a piece of non-existent dust. "Though I hate to sound pompous, there are not many experts in the country who have the skills necessary to unmask this as the forgery that it undoubtedly is."

"I understand," said Percy quietly.

He stared into her eyes as the hair on her neck bristled. "I shall expect a call from the police concerning this forthwith, and I would ask that you refer me as an expert witness." He narrowed his eyes. "If I do not receive such a call within forty-eight hours, I will be forced to report its existence to the police on my own. Do you understand?"

The irritating droplets of perspiration had spread to other locations and a nasty case of nausea was roiling her stomach. *Oh, Nigel! What were you involved in?*

"Certainly." She reached for the picture, but Mr. Grace put his hand out to stop her.

"I cannot emphasize the gravity of the situation enough, Mrs. Pontefract. As a guardian of the purity of the sacred works of art left to the world by long-dead masters, I have a responsibility to report this to the authorities. Indeed, I would say it is an oath. However, as an act of good faith, I am allowing *you* to take the painting to the police."

75

She pulled the print toward her and placed it back in the unremarkable brown bag. "I assure you I do understand the gravity of the situation, Mr. Grace. That is why I asked to see you."

They both stood and she reached out a hand. He peered at it as if her hand were a large spider, then gave it a limp shake. "I shall be hearing from you."

"Of course." As she made for the door, her coat caught on the arm of the chair, and she had to yank it free.

"One more thing, Mrs. Pontefract," he said as he rounded the desk, eyes fixed on the bag.

"Who *is* the talented artist?"

She hesitated, thinking how best to word her answer. "I am afraid he is deceased. If the police do believe this to be the product of criminal activity, I am sure they will disclose his name. Good day."

Chief Inspector Thompson held the painting between his arms, turning it this way and that.

"It's a Vermeer. Well, a copy," explained Percy.

"I'm not a complete neanderthal, Mrs. Pontefract," said the handsome inspector, giving her a dirty look that veered into a smile.

"I didn't mean to suggest you were, Chief Inspector," she assured him, "but not everyone is familiar with the piece."

"My mother has a coffee table book on famous art," he explained.

Percy straightened her shoulders. "I have come straight from an art appraiser with all the right credentials, and he has authenticated that it is an excellent forgery. A Mr. Grace. He is expecting your call."

"And you found this in all those pictures at your cousin's flat," he confirmed.

She nodded. "My cousin mentioned that he wanted to show me his other styles of art, but he died before he had the chance. When his mother found out his intentions, she gave me the key."

The chief inspector tutted and shook his head. "I'll have to have a word with those country boys. How could they have missed it?"

"In their defense, it was hidden among a mass of other original works. I almost missed it myself."

She placed the crumpled, soiled receipt on the inspector's desk.

"Phew! That's a lot of money!" he declared.

"Do you see this number?" she asked, pointing to the faint digits on the paper. "Turn the canvas over and look at the frame."

The inspector did as she suggested, and squinting, looked along the whole frame. "Not seeing anything."

Percy came up beside him, very conscious that she was taller, and pointed to the hardly legible pencil number. "See! Right there. It's the previous number in the series."

The inspector followed her finger then looked back at the receipt.

"One-hundred and forty-eight!" he shouted. Percy jumped out of her skin at his impassioned response. He marched around the room, pulling his hair. "You're telling me that your cousin had forged and sold one hundred and forty-seven forgeries?"

His fiery mood was making her nervous. "I'm not telling you anything, Chief Inspector. I don't know if that's what the numbers indicate, but at least now you have a trail to follow."

"Give me that telephone number!" he demanded, his patrician features rippling with anger.

She cocked her head with a frown. She was not the criminal here.

"I apologize," he said, controlling his tone. "It's not your fault that we are on the brink of the biggest scandal to ever hit the art world. Would you please give me the art appraiser's telephone number?"

She reached into her commodious bag looking for Mr. Grace's number, wishing she had simply put it in her pocket. "It's in here somewhere," she said with a grimace. "Just a moment." Her finger hit the sharp-edged brooch. She had forgotten all about it.

"Oh, and I found this on the floor in Nigel's flat." She placed it deliberately on the desk.

The chief inspector picked up the shiny jewel, examining it. "Did you have this appraised too?"

She laughed, nervously. "No! I don't suppose it's real, but it does mean there was a woman in his flat. He had paintings of several of them."

Holding it close, he asked, "Where exactly did you say you found it?"

She hadn't. Deliberately. Percy felt her cheeks heat as she continued her hunt for the telephone number. "Under his bed."

"Indeed," said the chief inspector with a smirk. "I didn't think he had a girlfriend."

"Neither did I." She poked her head into her bag. "Got it!"

She waited as the inspector used his black, utilitarian telephone to call the art expert.

"Please tell Mr. Grace that Chief Inspector Thompson of Scotland Yard is calling." There was a pause. "Yes, this is Chief Inspector Thompson. I understand you appraised a painting brought to you by a Mrs. Pontefract this morning."

As the inspector listened, he nodded a great deal. "I understand the ramifications, sir. I regret to inform you that since this painting is evidence in an ongoing murder investigation, I cannot give out any information regarding the artist at this time."

Though Percy could not hear the sedate voice of the man on the other end of the line, she wondered at his reaction to the word 'murder'. She had not come close to suggesting it.

Quiet for a moment, the chief inspector's face unreadable, he eventually said, "As I have already said, I cannot comment. I am merely calling to confirm that the quality of this painting is that of an excellent forgery meant to deceive the general public."

He listened for a moment more. "You may be called as an expert witness if this case goes to trial. Are you prepared to fill that duty?" Satisfied, he placed the receiver in its cradle.

"Well, this is a fine mess," Thompson said with a sigh. "And it takes my investigation in a whole new direction."

# Chapter 11

Percy was on her way to London by train for the opening of a new art exhibit at the Charing Gallery.

The only people she hadn't really managed to talk to since the murder were Lord Banbury and Sir William Packett. It had taken every ounce of courage and determination she could muster, but holding her nose, she had called her mother, since one of her hobbies was reading the society pages and magazines as if they were religious texts—if anyone knew where the two men were likely to show up, it was Doris Crabtree.

After having to endure another impassioned rant about the imminent road construction, Percy asked her mother if she knew anything about Sir William.

"What a gentleman he was," said her mother in a wistful tone. "It's not often that the gentry make time for those of us of lower status." That was not quite how Percy remembered him, but if it mellowed her mother's mood, she was willing to let the fib fly. "Why do you want to know?"

Percy had given much thought to this question with Mrs. Appleby over dinner the night before and was ready with her contrived answer. "Agatha gave me a key to Nigel's flat, and I found quite a few unsold paintings. I thought Sir William might be interested in some of them before they go on sale to the general public."

"Is it more of those atrocious abominations?" her mother asked.

"A lot of them, yes," Percy replied, omitting the fact that more of them were traditional.

"I do *not* know what people see in that tripe. There's no accounting for taste, I suppose," spat out her mother.

"So?"

"Can't you get his number from the exchange?" asked Mrs. Crabtree.

"I hardly think they are at liberty to give out the telephone numbers of the nobility, Mother. No, I thought I'd try to bump into him at some public event. Much more natural."

"There is a new painting being unveiled at the Charing Gallery and they actually quoted Sir William. It caught my eye because he is a *personal* friend."

Though sorely tempted, Percy did not have time to laugh about the imaginary world her mother had fabricated to soothe her pride which was always bent by lack of a title. "When is it?"

"Wednesday, I think. Let me check."

Percy held a blissfully silent phone while her mother tracked down the article.

"Here it is. Yes, Wednesday, doors open to the public at ten."

"Thank you. I don't suppose you've been keeping similar tabs on Lord Banbury, have you?"

"As a matter of fact…" Percy could hear the rustling of paper. "A new statue commemorating those in the Second Boer War is to be unveiled in Whitehall on Friday and Lord Banbury is one of the sponsors."

"And what time is that?" asked Percy, scribbling the information down.

"Two o'clock in the afternoon. Perhaps I'll join you. It is only proper to support our important new acquaintances."

A black sack draped over Percy's head by a violent criminal could not have made her feel more despair than those few words. She cursed her inability to think on her feet. "Ah, Friday? I'm not sure I can make it Friday. I have plans." She clenched her jaw and scrunched an eye shut, waiting to see the effect of her declaration.

"Well, I could go alone, I suppose. Let me check the weather." Percy crossed her fingers that it would be stormy. Her mother couldn't abide the rain, since she had the same wiry hair as her daughter and spent much time and money wrestling it into obedience. Mrs. Crabtree's vanity would not allow her to be in the same area as Lord Banbury, and who knew what other dignitaries, with frizzy locks.

"Humph! Rain all day."

"Too bad," said Percy with a secret grin, barely refraining from dancing a jig. "I shall just have to catch Lord Banbury another time. If you see his name pop up again, can you leave a message with Mrs. Appleby?"

"I *shall* not," announced her mother. "I will call until I reach *you*. You are much too familiar with that cook, Persephone. You must keep the boundaries between the classes, or they will begin to take advantage."

As green fields and colorful villages flew by the train window, the irony of this phrase kept Percy smiling for a long time.

When the train finally squealed to a stop in London, Percy adjusted her hat and gloves before stepping down onto the platform amidst the crowds. Working her way through to the curb, she hailed a taxi and checked her watch. In order not to miss Sir William, she had come an hour early.

Stepping out in front of the art museum, she saw a short queue had already assembled and joined the back. A poster heralded the arrival of the newly acquired painting, a Rembrandt, that had gone up for auction after the death of the owner.

Within fifteen minutes, the queue had doubled in length, and she was thankful she had resisted the urge to ignore her alarm. By the time the museum doors were due to open, she could no longer see the end of the line.

Pushing through into a circular, Grecian foyer with mosaic flooring, she grabbed a guide from a uniformed usher and shuffled her way to the exhibit. The Rembrandt was a large picture, covered by a red velvet curtain with a gold rope pull. Ropes had been placed to cordon off the area immediately around the painting, and fortunately she found herself in the second row. For once she was grateful for her almost six-foot height.

A glance at her watch showed that the unveiling would occur in ten minutes. She felt a shove from behind and slammed into the small woman in front of her, who fell forward and sent the flimsy barrier tumbling. The woman shot her a hot glare of accusation, but Percy just shrugged and pointed behind, then helped the grumbling woman to her feet.

As the ushers were resurrecting the barrier, a small group of people were escorted in, one being Sir William Packett sporting his monocle. Percy relaxed.

The museum curator made some opening remarks, then ceded the floor to Sir William.

"It is with many thanks that I accept the privilege of revealing this outstanding work from an Old Master. As a member of the nobility of this great country I feel an obligation to enrich its coffers with works of outstanding beauty and value when it is within my power to do so. I am proud to have played an instrumental part in securing this particular piece for the enjoyment of all citizens."

A smattering of applause followed his remarks.

"So, without further ado, I give you *The Storm* by Rembrandt, painted in 1633." Sir William gave the gold cord a little tug, and the curtain began to sweep back to reveal the three-hundred-year-old painting. Clapping, coupled with quiet cheers of approval, filled the atrium.

Percy looked toward where Sir William was standing and was disappointed to see a crowd had already gathered around him. Some were obviously press photographers, and others, art enthusiasts. She stood on the outskirts, biding her time.

After five minutes had passed, Sir William happened to look up, and they locked eyes. The monocle fell against his chest. She could tell he recognized her but could not place from where. He nodded as if to say he would get to her. A further ten minutes later, the crowd around him lost interest, and he stepped toward Percy with a frown.

"I know we have met…" He extended a hand.

"My cousin, Nigel Fotherington. The art exhibit at your gallery."

Comprehension flooded his weathered features. "Ah, yes. Your interest in art goes beyond your own family, then?"

"Oh, yes! When I saw the advertisement about this I just *had* to come." She crossed her fingers behind her back.

Sir William ran a little finger across the top of his lip. "That was a sad business about your cousin. Have the police made any progress?"

"I was in contact with the chief inspector just a few days ago, and there *has* been a development. Nigel's flat was filled with unsold paintings."

A glint sparkled in Sir William's eye, though if it were from concern or excitement, Percy could not tell.

"Are they like those in the exhibit?" he asked, wiry eyebrows trembling in anticipation.

"Not at all. They are far more conventional," she explained. "Am I to understand you are not familiar with that side of his work?"

Sir William's prominent chin dropped as he shook his head. "I was only privy to his latest, modern work which was brought to my attention by a mutual friend who understands my passion for fine art and especially that of new British artists. The friend came to my home with an example of Nigel's work, and I knew it was just the right style for the gallery. I wrote to invite your cousin to exhibit at the opening and offered to cover the costs."

"Did you meet Nigel before the exhibition?" she asked.

84

After the slightest of hesitations, he said, "No. I was impressed enough with the sample. We arranged everything over the phone."

"If you don't mind me asking," Percy began, "how were you to recoup the advance?"

"From the sales of the paintings. Nigel had a contract written up by a London solicitor which I signed before the exhibit. Your cousin was extraordinarily talented. His death is a tragedy for the world of art. It is quite possible that he could have become a British Van Gogh." He adjusted the cuffs of his shirt which shone with gold cufflinks. "I say, do you think I could have a look at his more traditional paintings, or are they part of the investigation?"

"I couldn't say," she replied. "You should call the chief inspector. They're still in the flat, considered evidence, but perhaps you could get permission. You might ask Agatha for one as compensation for fronting him the money."

"I haven't been to Hampshire in quite some time," responded the peer, fixing the monocle in his eye. "It's lovely this time of year."

Percy felt a punch in the gut. She had not mentioned that Nigel lived in Hampshire.

# Chapter 12

"How did Sir William know Nigel lived in Hampshire if he claimed not to know him before the exhibit?" said Mrs. Appleby as she peeled potatoes into a sieve.

"That, Mrs. A, is the question. That fact has shot him to the top of my suspect list. If Hampshire wasn't so far, I would go and do some blasted surveillance."

"Don't you know someone closer who could do it for you?" the cook said as she cut the potatoes into chunks on a battered, wooden chopping board and tipped them into the pot, half filled with salty water.

"No, I don't know—" Percy slapped her forehead. "Yes, I do! Nigel lived over a shop. A shoe shop. I could call them, if only I can remember the name." She jumped up and started to pace, her neck pushed forward like a pigeon. "What was it called? Potiffers? Pumpfords?" She shook her head. "Come on brain! Think!" Pacing again she tried more names. "Pickfords? Palmers?"

"Powells?" suggested Mrs. Appleby as she took the pot with both hands over to the Aga.

"Porters!" cried Percy in triumph. "I'll call and ask them to keep an eye out. Fortunately, Sir William Packett is not a run-of-the-mill man and will be easy to identify."

"As long as he doesn't dress up in disguise," murmured the cook, pulling some carrots from a basket.

"You can't disguise that plummy accent. No, if he shows up, they'll be sure to notice."

Percy pushed into the hall and asked the exchange to put her through to the shoe store.

"Mr. Porter," said Percy in the most soothing voice she could muster. "I don't know if you remember me? Mrs. Pontefract, cousin of Nigel Fotherington?"

"Of course, of course. Such a tragedy. What can I do for you?"

"I was surprised to see quite a collection of art still in Mr. Fotherington's apartment when I was there. I am sure you know that paintings are far more valuable when the artist is dead, and I am worried that someone might try to steal some of them. Hampshire is so far from where I live which makes overseeing the works problematic, but I was wondering if you and your staff might be able to keep an eye on any comings and goings?"

"It would be a privilege, Mrs. Pontefract. Should I call the police if I see any strangers?"

"Oh, no. That won't be necessary. Just let me know and I can contact them. I cannot thank you enough, Mr. Porter. Thank you so much."

She hung up the phone feeling rather proud of herself.

Friday was overcast just as the forecast had predicted, but the rain had fallen while Percy was on the train, leaving the air damp but not wet. Her hair had given her a particularly hard time that morning, and she had spent far too long grappling with it to no avail. In the end, she had pinned it up with so many clips that the frizz would be completely hidden under her hat.

Westminster was bustling as usual, and she experienced the same thrill she always did when close to the seat of government. Big Ben struck one which meant she had plenty of time to get to the new memorial. She strolled past the beautiful Gothic Revival Palace that was home to the House of Commons and Lords then crossed the street to pop into Westminster Abbey. She enjoyed the stained glass and seeing the names in Poet's Corner.

When she emerged, the sky had turned a dark gray, and she dug into her copious bag to ensure she had brought the new-fangled, telescopic umbrella. *There it was.* She cut across the green and followed the road to Whitehall, passing the King's Guards. A small crowd was beginning to assemble around a statue shrouded in canvas. She shimmied her way to the front which caused some complaints because of her height. To accommodate the grumblers, she bent her knees.

It started to spit with rain, but in the crowd, she was loathed to put up an umbrella and hoped it would not get worse. Within ten minutes, a gaggle of men in suits and hats approached, shooting worried glances at the sky and crowding under the statue. Among them was Lord Banbury.

Percy raised a gloved hand to shoulder-height in greeting and Lord Banbury nodded in recognition just as the sounds of a military band struck up. Percy looked to the left and saw the soldiers marching, their brass instruments brilliant even in the gloom, the music staccato and patriotic. They stopped and marched in front of the statue for several moments, their boots crunching on the road, then circled and came to rest behind the officials as the last bars were played.

An older gentleman, his chest heaving with medals, stepped forward and began a speech about the Second Boer War and those valiant men who had died. His delivery was dry, and Percy's mind wandered as she surreptitiously watched Lord Banbury in her peripheral vision. His gaze was fixed on the speaker, a rigid smile on his lips.

As the old soldier delivered the final lines, he thanked Lord Banbury and a host of other prominent men for their support. The crowd applauded, and then the soldier pulled a rope and the bronze statue of three men bent, rifles at the ready, was revealed.

A young woman brought an armful of evergreen wreaths and gave one to each of the men in the group. They laid the wreaths at the foot of the monument, and then the whole spectacle was over. Lord Banbury looked over his shoulder and walked toward her.

"You're Nigel Fotherington's cousin, aren't you?"

"Yes. Small world, isn't it?" She beamed, worrying she was overdoing it.

"Do you have an interest in the Boer War?" he asked, with his unusual emphasis on the letters 't' and 's'.

"Oh, not really. I came to town on business and noticed there was some kind of memorial happening and thought I'd stick around."

The small drops of rain fattened and smacked the pavement around them. Lord Banbury looked up at the angry clouds.

"I say, I have a few moments before I have to be anywhere. Can I buy you a cup of tea?"

"That would be lovely," she said and followed him to a tea shop on the corner.

As they pulled open the door, the heavens opened. "Good timing," he grinned. "That's why old Gallagher's speech was uncharacteristically short. We knew the rain was coming."

He shuffled her to a seat near the window and she watched as the rain streamed down the glass.

After ordering, he asked her, "Have the police made any progress?" The heavy stress on the last sound of the phrase made her think of a hissing snake.

"Not that I know of," she replied. "You're an enthusiast of the modern style, I understand."

He ran a hand over his bald pate. "I am a lover of *all* art; the Old Masters, the Impressionists, the Renaissance. I have an extensive collection in my home near Winchester."

*Winchester? Wasn't that in Hampshire?*

"Do you have a separate wing for the modern pieces?" she asked with a wink as the waitress placed their tea on the table.

His expression indicated that he understood her little jab. "I haven't actually taken the plunge yet. I was hoping to start my collection with something from your cousin, but it didn't seem appropriate after what happened."

"No, indeed." She took a sip, but it was too hot and burnt her tongue. She winced. "How did you hear about my cousin, if you don't mind me asking?"

Banbury slapped some milk into his cup. "I run in the same circles as Sir William, and he mentioned he was backing an up-and-coming, young artist to open his new gallery. He knows of my penchant and asked if I would be interested in coming to the opening. He said he would consider it a personal favor, as the presence of an earl would only help with publicity."

"Well, that was very nice of you." She pinched her lips into a tight smile and immediately stopped, horrified that it would make her resemble her mother.

"It was the least I could do. Sir William was very impressed with your cousin's work, and I value his opinion. He thought your cousin might crash onto the art scene and told me his early work might be a good investment."

"He was prepared to say that after only seeing a sample piece?" she asked.

Lord Banbury frowned. "Oh, no. I believe he had seen most of the pieces that would be on display at the exhibition."

*Strange.* "But *you* had not seen any of it before that night?"

"No. But it was…true to the style."

"Are you saying you didn't like it?" She tipped her head conspiratorially. "My mother absolutely hated it. It was rather fun seeing her discomfort that day."

"I wouldn't go so far as that. It's a new style—a revolt against the camera. Intended to shock. I daresay when our senses become accustomed, we will develop a taste for it."

"If that isn't the most polite way of saying you didn't like it, I don't know what is," she said with a laugh, trying to imagine the earl with a full head of hair.

He merely grinned in response, revealing unusually straight teeth.

"It was rather sporting of you to stay with the body until the police came. Poor Agatha was beside herself. It will take her a long time to recover."

"It was nothing," he said, flapping a soft hand. "As I said at the time, sadly, I have experience of death from two wars. I thought it better to save the ladies from the horror and know enough to understand that the police want to preserve the crime scene. That way if anyone came along the alley, I could stop them."

"Did anyone come along?"

"No. The neighboring shop owners poked their heads out, but no one else tried to come into the alley, which I thought was odd, as there is an outhouse that serves several of the businesses. I thought I'd have to ask them to find a public toilet."

"I saw him," Percy blurted out. "Nigel, I mean. Quite by accident."

Lord Banbury stopped stirring his tea. "Oh?"

"I was in the kitchen hallway and the door was ajar, and I could see poor Nigel—" She pushed the napkin to her mouth.

The earl's gray eyes looked into hers. "When was that?"

She flapped the napkin. "Oh, you know, sometime."

"Was it after the inspector arrived?" He had become rather serious.

Percy pulled her mouth down. "I really couldn't say. Does it matter?"

He smiled, but it held no warmth. "Not at all. I was merely making conversation." He sipped his tea and placed the cup carefully in the saucer. "What did you say your business was here today?"

They locked gazes. Percy felt her pulse kick up a notch. "I didn't."

He shook his head like a bird after a bath. "My head is in the clouds. I thought you mentioned it. No matter."

Feeling the need to diffuse the strained atmosphere, Percy dunked her biscuit in her cup. "Did you know that Nigel painted real pictures?"

The earl raised both brows. "Did he?"

"Yes. He was actually a very talented classical artist. I've seen some of them. There is one I would love to have as a keepsake."

The earl placed both hands on the tabletop. "I would be *very* interested to see them. Perhaps after the police finish their investigation, the pictures will be sold on the open market. Would you let me know?" He pulled a small silver compact out of his inside jacket pocket, and as he did so, a folded piece of paper fell to the floor between the window and the table. Lord Banbury appeared not to notice and, opening the silver case, handed her his card.

"Certainly," she said, willing herself not to look at the fallen paper.

The earl glanced at his watch, then at the sky outside. The cloudburst shower was over.

"It was lovely meeting you again, Mrs. Pontefract." He stood. "But I must get to my next appointment." He took her hand and kissed it. "Till we meet again."

She watched him cross the road and walk briskly along the opposite pavement. When she was sure he was out of sight, she leaned down to retrieve the fallen paper.

*Saturday 4pm. Duke of Wellington.*

The whole thing was written in shockingly familiar block capitals.

The Pontefract farmhouse was filled with the comforting smell of Irish stew when Percy arrived home that evening. Throughout the journey on the train, she had stared at the note and its deadly implications. Did peers murder people? She thought she remembered Lord Banbury in the gallery when Cecily had burst in screaming. But could she be sure he was present before that?

After removing her hat and coat she found Mrs. Appleby in the kitchen putting the final touches on a fruit cake.

"Hello, Mrs. Pontefract. How was London?" The cook had a smudge of flour on her forehead.

"Interesting." Percy lowered herself slowly into a chair.

"Oh? Here, let me serve you some stew and mashed potatoes and you can tell me all about it."

Mrs. Appleby pulled the casserole dish from the oven and placed it in the middle of the oak table. The thick gravy was happily bubbling at the edges, and Percy was gratified to see soft, white dumplings floating in the brothy sauce.

The cook ladled a healthy amount of stew into a bowl and cut a thick doorstop of local bread to go with it. Percy tore the slice apart and dipped the spongy goodness into the rich gravy. After serving her own portion, Mrs. Appleby said, "Now, what was so interesting?"

Percy told her about her awkward conversation with Lord Banbury and the discovery of the note in the same handwriting as the one that may have lured Nigel into the alley and to his death.

"Just because Nigel got a note does not mean the person who sent it is the one who killed him," Mrs. Appleby pointed out. "It could have been a perfectly innocent meeting or an old note."

An invisible weight lifted from Percy. "Why didn't I think of that? I had Lord Banbury arrested, charged and convicted already."

"It could be suspicious, to be sure, but not conclusive, by any means. His Lordship was there to buy a painting, correct? He may have wanted to talk to Nigel in private about a fair price."

Percy grabbed the notebook which was still on the table and recorded the presence of the note next to Lord Banbury's name. She held her pencil above the page. "There is one more thing."

Mrs. Appleby cocked a brow.

"He lives in Hampshire."

The cook's forehead knitted.

"Nigel lived in Hampshire," Percy explained, waving her hands for dramatic emphasis.

A large smile crept across the older woman's face. "If living in Hampshire is incriminating then you have a pretty big list of suspects."

Percy sighed. "You know what I mean. If you put that together with the fact that he was at the exhibition and his handwriting seems to match the note found on Nigel, that makes *three* incriminating facts."

The phone began to ring in the hall.

"Shall I get it?" asked Mrs. Appleby.

Percy thought of her mother's reprimand and her promise to call if she saw Lord Banbury's name attached to another event.

"I'll get it. It could be Piers."

The cook's face fell. "I forgot. He already called. He had to go up North. He won't be back until the weekend."

"Oh." Percy felt disappointment slosh in her chest. "Still, I'll get it. I'm expecting a call from Mother."

She braced herself and headed toward the telephone much like a soldier might approach boot camp.

"Fetching 548."

"Mrs. Pontefract?" The cockney accent surprised her. "It's Syd. Syd Smythe, the waiter from the gallery. I need to see you."

# Chapter 13

Percy was on her third trip to London in as many weeks. Syd had been very 'cloak and dagger' in the phone call and had asked to meet her far from the art gallery at a pub in Greenwich. After getting off the train, she took a taxi which dropped her outside the *Bucket of Blood* public house. Once a red brick building, its windows were grimy with soot, the wooden sills fluttering with flaking paint.

She took a deep breath.

Choking on all the smoke inside, Percy waited a moment for her eyes to adjust to the dim interior. The dingy room was full of older men in tatty work clothes and dusty flat caps, all eyes on her. Moving slowly forward so as not to trip under the pressure of so many harsh witnesses, she swung her gaze from side to side for sight of Syd.

Just as she was about to give up hope and make a run for it, she saw a cap waving from the back, the young waiter grinning from a table in a dark corner.

"Thanks for coming, Missus," he said. "What you drinkin'?"

She raised a hand in protest, casting an apprehensive glance at the sticky table. "Oh, I'm fine. Not thirsty."

"Sure?" His artful face was doubtful.

"Absolutely. Now what can I do for you Mr. Smythe?" The sooner she got out of here the better.

The grin slid off his face like oil off a fresh batch of chips. "I didn't tell the police everythin' I saw," he began, pulling at his collar as if it were strangling him.

She frowned. "Whyever not?"

He placed both hands around the pint glass. "Well, I might 'ave 'ad some dealings with the coppers in the past what 'as made me…'ow shall I say? Cautious." He winked.

"I understand," she said, realizing too late that she hadn't checked the chair before sitting down. Was it naïve to hope it was clean? *Blast!* She prayed her coat would not cleave itself to the seat. "And you want to ask my advice?"

"Somethin' like that, yeah." He leaned back and looked at her so hard she began to feel a little uncomfortable.

"Why me?" she asked.

"Well, I can't tell no toffs, and the older ladies turned their noses up at me, I could tell. That skinny bloke too and the sister who was a wreck. That leaves you. You seem like a nice lady."

Her suspicious mind was alive with scenarios. Was he trying to butter her up? Was he going to ask her for money? Was he the murderer? *Calm down, Percy.*

She put her hands together and laid them on the table but immediately regretted it. She looked in her purse for a hankie and made a decision. "Alright. Tell me what you know. I'll try to help."

"I told the copper I didn't see nothin'," he began. "Always best not to get involved when the police arrive, in my experience. They kicked me out of the kitchen so they could use it for interviews, and I sat wiv my back against the wall, eyes closed as if I couldn't care less." He winked again. "But I 'ad seen things and was very interested in everyone. My eyes weren't really closed. They were 'ardly open, but I could see *everyone.*"

Percy's pre-occupation with the squalor of her surroundings waned, and her curiosity began to wake up.

Syd's hands were fiddling with the grubby beer mat. "I was in and out of the kitchen refillin' the trays—you lot can eat, I'll say that! And I kept passin' men in that narrow 'allway. There was an outhouse shared by several of the shops in the alley and to the left a bit, but I felt like a fish swimming upstream 'alf the time."

Percy remembered the earl mentioning an outhouse. She had not known about it at the time of the exhibit. She tried to imagine her mother or the dowager using such primitive facilities and couldn't.

"Well, not long before Mr. Fotherington's sister starts yelling, I 'ear 'im outside with someone."

A familiar rush of adrenalin ran through her veins. "Who? Nigel? Did you see who it was?" Forgetting the filthy condition of the table, she leaned her elbows on it.

Syd's face fell a little. "Not really. It was definitely a bloke 'cause I could 'ear muffled talkin', but I couldn't actually see 'im."

"A man." That halved her list.

"Yeah. I didn't think much of it, and I was so busy with the food and everythin', but when I sat against the wall wiv my eyes 'alf shut, I remembered it." He leaned toward her. "And that's not all."

Percy felt her eyes grow larger as the young man continued his confessions. Had he seen her snooping around in the kitchen?

"I went to get a knife to 'elp me open a stubborn bottle of champagne, and I noticed one was missing."

Relief washed over her. "When was that?"

"About 'alf an hour before the poor chap was discovered."

This was interesting indeed.

Syd squinted a youthful eye like the old men around him. "And what was a posh lady like 'is sister doing in the alley in the first place, eh?"

This was a valid question that she had not considered. What was Cecily doing among the dustbins? Syd's musings were making Percy feel rather lacking in the detection department, but she justified her failings by reminding herself that she was rather sozzled at the time.

"That is a good point, Sydney. A very good point."

"Sydney's my dad. Just call me Syd."

And in an unexpected moment of clarity, she remembered it was Bernard Partridge, future KC, who had been absent for a while before his wife began to scream.

The unreachable memory had finally come into focus. Could it be him Syd heard in the alley with Nigel?

"Since they still 'aven't collared anyone for 'is murder, do you think I should tell the coppers any of this?" He rubbed the end of his nose for the umpteenth time. "I really don't wanna."

"If you like, *I* can tell the chief inspector that an anonymous source told me the information." Nonetheless, whatever Syd thought of the man, Chief Inspector Thompson was no fool. He would connect the dots. "But I cannot guarantee he won't want to talk to you—though I will discourage it."

Syd's energetic eyes narrowed. "'E'll ask why I didn't tell 'im the first time, and I'll get in trouble. I don't want no trouble."

"Of course, you don't. I'll ask the inspector to go easy on you, if it comes to that." She pushed her chair back to leave. "Why are you telling me now, Syd? So long after the fact?"

"I feel bad for Mr. Fotherington. 'E was nice to me and gave me a pound tip. It's been eatin' at me. One good turn deserves another, don't it?"

Percy nodded then had a thought. "Syd, don't be tempted to earn money by sniffing around and telling suspects you have dirt on them. That is a dangerous business."

"No worries there Mrs. P. My cousin went to see 'is Maker two years ago after trying to blackmail someone. Cured me of all such desires, I can tell you."

She was surprised when Syd jumped up and came round the table to pull out her chair.

"Thanks again for coming and listenin' to me. I feel like a ruddy great weight 'as been lifted."

"Not at all," she said as she tore the coat fabric from whatever substance it had stuck to.

As she weaved her way back through the tables, like a drowning man making for shore, she could not deny that the visit had been extremely valuable. Her mind was working overtime.

"Fancy making you go to a seedy place like that?" said Mrs. Appleby when Percy returned and showed her the state of the coat.

"Syd was nervous. He wanted to be far away from Chelsea. I'm sure he's of the school of thought that walls have ears."

"I think we'll have to send your coat out to be cleaned," Mrs. Appleby tutted.

"What he told me makes it all worthwhile," she assured the cook and divulged Syd's insights.

Mrs. Appleby filled the sink to wash some dishes. "Cecily was out in a dirty alley? What would she have been doing out there?"

"It's logical if you think about it. How could she have found her brother's body if she had *not* been out there? It irks me to think I didn't draw that conclusion before. I *was* a little woozy, but I certainly came to life when Cecily raised the roof. But what kind of detective am I if I didn't wonder why she was in the alley in the first place?"

"Go easy on yourself, Mrs. Pontefract," said Mrs. Appleby as she added washing soda to the warm water. "Everyone's in a fluster after a murder, I should imagine."

Percy tapped the table. "Apparently there was an outhouse, but I can't see Cecily using it. She's very particular. She would have gone to find a nice public lavatory. I know I would have, if I had needed to."

"I shudder at the thought of outhouses now, but it's what I grew up with," agreed Mrs. Appleby. "I'd rather walk a mile for one of those fancy underground places than subject myself to a lav."

Percy nodded and opened her notebook. "And if the knife had been removed thirty minutes before the murder, it leads me to the conclusion that this was no crime of opportunity. Too bad Syd didn't see who took it."

Hands still in the soapy water, Mrs. Appleby spoke over her shoulder. "Have you considered the possibility that maybe he did?"

Percy snapped up her head. "You think he only told me *some* of what he knew?" She reflected on his less-than-honest face. He had admitted to growing up on the wrong side of the law. Perhaps during his petty criminal activities he had developed the ability to lie without conscience.

But it didn't feel right.

"How would you rate his honesty?" asked the cook.

Percy pushed her lips to the side and grabbed her chin. "Not high. He admitted he is nervous of the police."

Mrs. Appleby turned around, a grim expression on her gentle face. "He could be the murderer, you know, and just set the whole thing up with you to muddy the waters. Who had greater access to the kitchen than Syd? I think you have to consider it."

Percy screwed up her face to consider Syd as the murderer. She hadn't felt like someone walked over her grave when Mrs. Appleby had made the suggestion. She snapped her fingers.

"Motive! Unless we can find a connection between Syd and Nigel, I cannot see why he would kill him."

Mrs. Appleby turned back to the sink with a shrug. "Well, if you don't like him for the murder, I still say he could be withholding information from you.

Percy tapped her lips. "I hope he doesn't do something stupid. I did warn him."

"So if Syd is telling you the truth, at least you know the murderer was a man. That's something." She placed a foamy mug on the drain.

"Something else has been bothering me," continued Percy. "Why hit Nigel over the head and *then* stab him?"

"Perhaps the knock on the head was just to stun him to make the stabbing easier."

Percy considered. "That is a reasonable explanation, Mrs. A." She absentmindedly drew an invisible circle on the oak table with her finger. "If it was a man Syd heard, then Cecily's trip to the alley was coincidence and had nothing to do with her brother's death. But I remembered who was missing while I was dozing. It was Bernard."

"Could Cecily have been trying to find her husband? Is all as rosy in the matrimonial garden as the couple want it to appear?" Mrs. Appleby grabbed a tea towel and began to dry the mugs.

"What do you mean?" asked Percy.

"I had a niece who married a man her parents weren't crazy about. Things went south pretty quickly, but my niece made a point of acting all smoochy in public. It was like that Shakespeare play—*'I think the lady doth protest too much'*. It was over the top. Made me suspicious, and I mentioned it to my sister. At first, she got upset at me for suggesting it, but when she thought it over, she had second thoughts and confronted her daughter alone. Turns out her husband was roughing her up. Could be the same thing here."

"I see what you're saying, but even if that's true, Mrs. A, I doubt it could be connected to Nigel's death."

Mrs. Appleby's lips puckered like she'd bitten into a lemon. Percy ignored her skepticism; she had no desire to suspect her cousin of her own brother's murder.

"With a shared outhouse in the alley, the killer took quite a risk," Mrs. Appleby mused.

"But the lavatory was the perfect excuse for going outside. Women generally hate them as we've said, so that's another indication that the killer was a man."

Percy flicked to a new page of the notebook after running an eye over her notes. "I'm not counting Uncle Frederick. That leaves Lord Banbury, who was rather odd when we had tea; Sir William Packett, who had a vested interest in Nigel's health since he had already put money into the venture, and Bernard." She bit the end of the pencil.

"You've left one off," said Mrs. Appleby, drying her hands.

Percy frowned. "Who?"

She cocked a gray brow. "Syd."

Percy wrinkled her nose. "If he's on the list I have to consider everything he told me a lie."

"Perhaps he was feeling you out to see what *you* knew. To see if you suspected him. He had access to the alley, the knives in the kitchen *and* the lead doorstop."

All of this was true. "And what would his motive be?"

Mrs. Appleby crossed her arms and leaned against the sink. "Perhaps he's in one of those gangs who just kill for sport."

"Do you really think that?" Percy asked.

"No, but you are too trusting, Mrs. Pontefract."

"Alright, I'll add Syd to the list, though it's against my better judgement."

She tapped the pencil on the table then slapped the tabletop with her palm. "We're forgetting the forgeries! That *has* to be why Nigel was killed. I just can't see how yet."

Mrs. Appleby had a hand firmly to her chest. "You just took ten years off my life!"

"Terribly sorry. I got excited."

"What if the forgeries were good enough to fool people who bought what they thought was the genuine thing? It would be galling to find out you had been taken," said Mrs. Appleby sitting on the opposite side of the table.

"That might make someone angry enough to kill," agreed Percy.

# Chapter 14

As Percy was fighting with her hair the next morning, she opened her jewelry box and chose a pin that would keep her floral scarf around her neck. As it glinted in the sunlight, she remembered the pretty brooch she had found under Nigel's bed. Since the chief inspector had not entered it into evidence and instead had left the ornament on his desk, she had reasoned that he did not regard the jewel as significant. She had popped it back into her bag before leaving his office, justifying her actions by promising herself that if the inspector asked for it in the future, she would gladly hand it over. But she had subsequently forgotten all about it.

Running downstairs, she rifled through her handbag and found the trinket. It was a pretty, silver butterfly with diamonds dotted on the wings. How could she find out to whom it belonged? She would first ask Agatha about the women at the funeral luncheon.

"Agatha?" she said into the phone. "It's Percy. How are you?"

"Percy, dear. I'd feel a lot better if the police knew who killed my poor boy. I'm not sleeping, I'm not eating. I'm going to waste away with grief."

Percy could not imagine the frustrating state of limbo in which Agatha currently found herself. "You poor thing!" she soothed. "I'm calling to let you know I went to Nigel's flat in Hampshire. I aired it out as you asked. He had a large inventory of incredible pictures—he was truly gifted—and there is one I'd particularly like to buy as a way to remember him."

"Oh, Percy, you can just have it," sniffed Agatha. "There are a lot of paintings, you say? I still haven't been able to bring myself to go over."

"Are you sure I can't pay for it? It was a smaller version of a much larger canvas. A seascape with a lighthouse. Do you know it?"

"No. Percy, I feel so guilty that I didn't take more interest in his work when he was alive…" A sob interrupted her flow. "I knew how talented he was and saw plenty of his work over the years, but I hadn't been over recently, and now I just can't seem to face it. I might ask Cecily to clear out the flat and then get some cleaners in. I've paid the next three months' rent, so I have time. As for the picture, think of it as a gift."

*Tricky.* "Um, that's very generous of you, Agatha. With regards to cleaning out the place, I would hold off until the police give you the all clear."

"The police? Why?" Agatha's voice sounded tense.

"Oh, you know, police stuff." What a dreadfully vague response. However, it was clear from Agatha's reaction that Chief Inspector Thompson had not yet contacted her about the forgery.

"By the way," she said hurriedly. "I found a brooch on the floor and want to return it to the owner. Nigel was in the middle of painting a portrait, and I recognized the woman as one of the ladies who came to your house after the funeral."

A subtle change in tone was the only indication of the importance Agatha attached to the find. "Really? What did she look like?"

"Brunette, blue eyes, heart-shaped face," replied Percy, listing off the pretty woman's features.

There was a pregnant pause. "Clara Trout." Agatha's words held an ounce of resignation. "Clara Montague now. She was the same age as Nigel, and they grew up playing together. She did rather well for herself and married a baronet. She's actually Lady Quinn."

*Lady Quinn?* "Can you give me her number? I'd like to return the brooch."

Though not as grand as the dowager's estate, Lady Quinn's manor house was not half bad. Made of beige stone, it sat in a valley surrounded by rolling, emerald meadows. Agatha was right; Clara had done well for herself.

A servant led Percy to a quaint parlor decorated in pink velvet and Percy wandered the room while she waited. A basket full of incomplete embroidery work sat next to an appealing lady's armchair. An oak occasional table housed a half-finished puzzle and a wireless radio set sat in front of a dainty piano that held a photograph of a handsome young woman. Behind it, on the wall, was a traditional Chinese painting of a waterfall.

Percy rushed to the center of the room when the door opened.

Clara's startling, ocean-blue eyes held a note of anxiety, though her raven hair was styled to perfection in the latest fashion. Percy's mouth watered as she laid eyes on her cream chiffon and lace, day dress.

"Mrs. Pontefract. I am so glad you contacted me. I couldn't for the life of me remember where I might have lost my brooch." She stared into Percy's eyes as if searching for an important answer there. "Where did you find it?"

Percy offered the ornament on her open palm. "In Nigel's flat. I saw your portrait there. It's a shame it won't be finished."

The agitated blue eyes swam with tears. "Isn't it? Do you think his mother would let me buy it unfinished?"

"I'm sure she will. I'm getting a seascape I particularly liked. Of course, Agatha will want to keep some of the pictures for herself, but a portrait is an undoubtedly *personal* commission."

A tall maid entered with a delicate silver tray containing a brilliantly shining teapot and two elegant, bone china cups with matching saucers.

"Thank you, Maisie. I can take it from here." The maid bobbed a curtsey and left.

Clara looked up with a crooked smile as she poured. "I still can't get used to people curtseying to me."

"But you are a baroness. It is customary," replied Percy.

"Yes, but in my heart, I am still the ordinary girl from Middleton."

Percy doubted she was ever ordinary. "How did Nigel come to paint your picture?"

"I'm sure his mother told you we were childhood friends. I'd heard that he was trying to make a splash on the art scene and wanted to help an old acquaintance, if I could. My husband had been encouraging me to have my portrait painted for some time, so I called Nigel and he agreed. I began travelling to his flat about four months ago." Her voice caught on the last word.

"You have a lovely home," said Percy to give Lady Quinn time to gather her emotions.

"Yes, it has been in my husband's family for over two hundred years. He allowed me to redecorate parts of it. This is my favorite room, as it looks over the gardens in the back."

Taking the proffered cup of tea, Percy asked, "How did you meet your husband, if that is not too impertinent."

A sad smile curved Clara's lips. "Of course not. My parents saved to buy me a horse when I was young. I was a natural and became interested in everything about horses. My parents took me to a military dressage demonstration when I was twelve and I was hooked. We attended the display every year thereafter.

"When I was seventeen, Arthur, my husband, began performing in the equestrian pageants. He had a young daughter who came to watch, and I discovered he was a widower. It impressed me that he was so devoted to his daughter.

"When I turned twenty, Arthur surprised me by inviting me to join him and his daughter for tea after a display. I didn't even know he knew who I was. My mother encouraged it—and can you blame her? Arthur was charming, warm, kind, handsome…and fifteen years my senior. We courted for six months before he asked me to marry him."

"What a lovely story," said Percy, wondering if it would be considered rude to take three of the little cakes. She bit into a heavenly éclair, soft and crisp at the same time.

"Where did you say you found the brooch?" Clara's tone was tentative.

Why did people always ask her loaded questions when her mouth was full? Percy stopped chewing and tried to swallow but did not succeed. Smiling with streaming eyes, she took a quick swig of the tea to wash it all down. It was becoming a habit.

"In Nigel's flat," she wheezed.

"Any particular place?"

Was Lady Quinn prodding, fearful that if she did not address the situation head on, Percy would become a liability?

Percy pursed her lips and felt cream all over them. She quickly licked it off and said quietly, "Under the bed."

Lady Quinn's complexion matched the deep pink of the blooms on the shelf behind her, and she dropped her gaze. "You must think very ill of me."

"I don't think anything at all," said Percy. "It really is none of my business…unless it was the reason Nigel was killed."

The sapphire eyes flashed to Percy's face. "No!" She brushed a hand across her skirt. "You don't know Arthur. He is the gentlest of creatures, which is why I feel so ashamed. W-would you allow me to explain?"

108

Percy's mouth shrugged. "You are under no obligation to explain anything to me, Lady Quinn."

"I know, but I want to. They say confession eases the wretched soul."

Percy nodded and placed her teacup on the pie crust table, suddenly hungry for something other than cake.

"As we grew older, Nigel and I began to develop feelings for each other. One summer in particular, we fell in love. He was just developing his skills as a painter and was getting ready to go to university. I was heartbroken at the thought of him leaving, and he said, 'Let's get married then.' I was over the moon, but both our parents shot the idea down." Percy remembered the anxious pause in her conversation with Agatha.

"They told us we were too young," Clara continued. "That he needed to focus on his art, etc... Undeterred, Nigel made me a ring out of a daisy, and we made a secret promise to each other. He left for college shortly after.

"At first, Nigel returned every weekend. Then it slowed to every few weeks and eventually trickled to academic holidays. I wrote countless letters begging him to come, but he claimed to be busy, always on the cusp of greatness. I became angry, imagining him with all sorts of other girls in Oxford.

"When Arthur asked me to tea, I accepted as a way to make Nigel jealous, but it didn't work because he was never around. Arthur treated me well and was exceptionally attentive. He soothed my neglected heart, and I mistook my feelings of gratitude for love. I recognized that this was not the fiery passion I had felt for Nigel, but that heated affection had burned out quickly, for him at least. Like a spent match. The kind of love Arthur was offering was steady and dependable...and would raise me up in society.

"When Arthur asked me to marry him, I accepted." A jeweled finger brushed a tear from her cheek. "As soon as the announcement hit the papers, Nigel reappeared telling me to break it off. But I had changed. What did Nigel have to offer me? Certainly not the life of luxury I had grown accustomed to. Besides, his indifference to my feelings had cured me of the desire for hot, blazing love—it could not be trusted." Clara stared out of the window, lost in painful memories.

"I refused to end my engagement, punishing Nigel for his neglect."

Percy was scared to breathe and break the spell of revelation. She gripped the arms of her chair.

"Ten years passed," Clara resumed after a short pause. "I followed Nigel's career from afar, but he never seemed able to attain the success he hoped for. At the same time, my husband was getting older, and in spite of our efforts, we had not had any children. My stepdaughter, who I had grown to love as a mother, had become an adult and didn't need me anymore. I was depressed and restless.

"When Arthur suggested I get my portrait painted, I truly thought our patronage might help Nigel. I was lying, of course, but I convinced myself it was true." She clasped her hands together on her knees.

"The first time I saw Nigel's flat I laughed. It confirmed I had taken the wiser path. Nigel was stuck in relative poverty, and I had wealth, respect and a title. But as I sat for him, the hard shell I had created around my heart gradually melted, and the old feelings returned. We both resisted for a while. Nigel knew I would never leave my husband. Arthur fell from a horse three years ago, leaving him lame. He depends on me, needs my assistance." The lovely eyelashes fluttered, and Percy hung on her every word, the confections forgotten. "I owe him that much for his constant care and kindness. And I do still love him." Clara's fist went to her chest. "Just not with the same passion Nigel evoked."

Lady Quinn shook her head like a young filly. "When Nigel invited us to the opening exhibition of the gallery, I hid the invitation from my husband. That was a line I was unwilling to cross. When I heard Nigel was dead, my first emotion was relief, relief that I would no longer betray Arthur.

"Since then, I have cried many private tears." She swept the moisture from her face and looked at Percy with uneasy eyes. "Will you tell Arthur?"

"Of course not!" declared Percy. "I have merely come to return your brooch. If I am guilty of any ulterior motive, it was to determine if you were implicated in his murder. I felt I owed my cousin that."

Through a watery smile, Clara whispered, "I am not used to people, other than my husband, showing me kindness. Nothing prepares you for the resistance one must face when climbing to a higher social class than the one to which you were born. It is a ferocious jungle, full of pacing lionesses and leopards."

"Then I feel nothing but pity for you, Lady Quinn. And I can assure you that your secret is safe with me. You have my word." Though Percy suspected that Agatha harbored fears.

# Chapter 15

The garden was beginning to emerge from its winter slumber, and Percy needed some twine and seeds to get started on her vegetable garden. Dressed in a warm coat and sensible shoes, she went out to her trusty, beloved Ford. Opening the door, she looked up the road. They had been fortunate enough to buy an old farmhouse that sat on three acres, but the house itself was only set back from the country road about forty feet. Her gaze rested on the figure of a man walking his dog, a black and white sheep dog she did not recognize.

Sliding into the front of the car, she put her shopping bag on the passenger seat next to her. Pressing the starter, the car gurgled into action, and she bounced out of the gravel drive and onto the country road that would take her into Melford. Having received a delightfully newsy letter from William while eating a hearty breakfast, she was feeling exceptionally optimistic about the day.

She passed the man with the dog as he turned onto a side road. Something about him struck her as familiar, but she shot past without seeing his face and was soon distracted by considering what she wanted to plant this year. After a mile, the road to Melford became a series of hills and dips. When the children were in the car they loved to holler and shout as the automobile plunged, making their stomachs jump. Today though, she was alone, and since the weather was rather foggy, she traversed the road at a more sedate pace.

Without warning, as Percy crested the first hill, a deer appeared out of the mist like an apparition. She slammed her foot to the brake. *Nothing.* Panicking, she swerved, successfully missing the deer, and pumped the brake. *Still nothing.* Heart in her throat, a cold sweat sweeping her entire body, she gripped the steering wheel, praying there were no other obstacles ahead. Anticipating a natural reduction in speed as the road eventually crept up once more, she braced. However, as she hurtled downward, a flash of red broke through the mist like a fiery meteor. Percy swerved the wheel hard to the left. The little, old car catapulted off the road, and Percy screamed, closing her eyes tight as a large oak tree loomed ahead. Bouncing down the rough embankment, her stomach flipped completely over as a last, violent bump pitched the nose of her beloved vehicle sharply down. *Smack!* Pain stabbed her forehead for a second before gravity plunged her vehicle into a deep ditch that ran in front of the ominous tree. Opening her eyes, chest resting on the steering wheel, she saw that the car was tipped forward on its nose, boot in the air like a French chorus girl.

"Hello! I say! Are you alright?" A concerned voice materialized out of the fog.

"Over here!" Percy squeaked while evaluating how badly she was hurt. Every breath made her wince with savage pain. Raw fear flowed unchecked through her veins, head throbbing with each beat of her heart. Attempting to move, she was prevented by the forces of physics as the Ford balanced on its front end. *Trapped!*

A rapid crunching of leaves and sticks heralded the fast approach of someone running and sliding down the steep slope. "Oh, my heavens!" the person cried, and Percy recognized it as the voice of the village librarian, Gilda Moncrief.

"Gilda! It's me! Percy!" Her voice was weak and strangled.

"Percy? How terrible. I'm so sorry. I didn't hear you coming. This is all my fault." She was fiddling with the damaged door.

"No! S-something was wrong with m-my brakes," responded Percy, her voice a little stronger. "Can you open the door?"

"Oh dear! It's all mangled. Can you push while I pull?"

Between them, they managed to pry the door open enough for Percy to fall out onto the leaf-strewn ground. Gilda gripped Percy's shoulders to lift her, but she was too heavy for the tiny woman. Instead, Percy pushed with her hand, gasping with sharp pain, until she was sitting, then rolled onto her knees and stood.

Her head spun furiously, and Percy plonked back down on the ground.

"You're bleeding!" cried Gilda. "Here, let me get a handkerchief."

Percy put a hand to her head, touching a sticky substance. She pulled her fingers down, covered in blood, and felt the bitterness of bile in her throat. She let herself fall to her side.

Golda pushed a folded handkerchief against the gash, and Percy took in deep, painful breaths until her stomach settled.

"Did you say your brakes didn't work?" asked the librarian.

"Yes. I pumped and pumped but to no avail."

"Do you think you can walk?" Gilda asked.

Percy's mouth shrugged as her head pounded. "I'm not sure."

Gilda put out her arm and Percy pushed on it until she was upright, the poor librarian almost falling herself under the weight. Percy's knees began to buckle, and she leaned on the little woman even harder.

After lingering for Percy to summon her strength, they managed to scramble slowly up the steep embankment to the road.

"My cottage is only two hundred yards from here," said Gilda once they reached the top. "Let me take you home for a cup of tea. You're in shock. Then I can call a tow truck and a doctor."

Percy's lip trembled. "Alright. I do feel a bit wobbly."

114

They tottered along the road until the familiar white fence and friendly yellow front door of Gilda's modest cottage swam into view. Percy lurched at the fence for support then shuffled into the cottage.

"I'll call the garage first then brew some tea. Come and sit in my parlor, Percy."

Gilda installed Percy in an uncomfortable wing-backed chair and disappeared. Percy put a hand up to sweep the frizzy hair out of her aching eyes and noticed that her bloody hand was trembling. She grabbed it with the other.

*She could have been killed.*

Suddenly the throbbing of her head intensified, sending unbearable pain radiating around her skull and behind her eyes.

Percy could hear Gilda on the phone giving directions to the only garage in the village. She leaned her aching head against the back of the stiff chair.

She should call Mrs. Appleby.

*She should call Piers.*

Her eyes began to sting. She didn't even know where he was. Piers had been away on business for the last three days. An overwhelming yearning to be enfolded in his arms crushed her, and a fervent sob bubbled out of her throat.

"Oh, dearie," said Gilda, pushing into the room holding a tray. Her empathy opened the floodgates. "There, there. Bob Sagebrush is coming to pull your car out of the ditch, and I've brought a nice cup of sweet tea and a couple of aspirin."

Percy took a shuddering breath and pressed the stained handkerchief to her runny nose.

"You've got…" Gilda pointed to Percy's face. "It's blood from your head."

Opening the hankie to find a clean spot, Percy rubbed her face.

"That's better," said Gilda.

"Could I use your telephone to call home?" Percy asked.

"Of course." Gilda watched as Percy struggled to her feet and limped into the hall. Muscles she didn't know existed were beginning to ache.

"Fetching 548."

"Mrs. A," said Percy in a shaky voice. "I've had a bit of an accident."

"Accident?" cried the faithful cook, her voice laced with fear. "Are you alright?"

"I'm alive but—" her voice cracked, and it took a moment to regain her composure as Mrs. Appleby listened in uncharacteristic silence. "I do have some bumps and bruises."

"Great heavens!" shrieked Mrs. Appleby. "How can we get you home and put you to bed?"

"Actually, could you have Piers call me? I'm not sure where he is but if you call the office—"

"I'll get right on it. Where are you?" demanded Mrs. Appleby.

"Gilda Moncrief's." She gripped her side. "The number is 224. And thank you."

"I'll be right down after I call Mr. Pontefract. It will only take me ten minutes to walk."

Percy replaced the telephone receiver, and every bone and muscle in her body revolted. She began to weep. *I need that aspirin.* She shuffled back to the parlor.

"Everything set?" asked Gilda as Percy swallowed down the pills with a gulp of tea.

"Mrs. Appleby is coming after she contacts my husband."

Gilda chuckled. "We sometimes wonder if you make him up."

Percy frowned. "He *is* gone a lot with his job, I admit, but I assure you he is real." The sticky sweet tea was beginning to perform its calming magic. "I keep reliving the moment I careened off the road—"

116

"Now, don't do that. It will make you feel giddy. Let's talk about something else to take your mind off it. How are your boys?"

Though Percy felt as though her body had been passed through a wringer, she told the librarian about the things she had done before the boys went back to school.

The phone rang.

"I'll get that," said Gilda.

Percy ran a hand over her raw eyes, willing the aspirin to work.

"It's Mr. Pontefract," Gilda said with a wink. "I guess he does exist."

Percy's body felt unusually heavy as she pushed herself up again and waddled back into the tiny hallway.

"Piers."

"Darling! Are you hurt? What happened?" His anxious concern turned on the waterworks, and through her sniffles, she told Piers what had happened.

"You think the brakes failed? But I had them checked not a month ago."

"Well, I pumped and pumped and nothing happened. Oh Piers, it was awful."

"Look, I'm back in London. I'm going to jump on the first train out. I should be there in less than two hours. Can you hold on till then, darling?"

Overcome with fear, shock, pain and emotion, she could hardly speak and merely moaned through the line.

"I'm leaving right now," he reiterated. "I love you."

"I love you too," she mouthed, replacing the phone.

He was coming.

By the time Piers arrived, Percy was installed in their bed, propped up with fluffy pillows and a generous portion of apricot crumble and custard. In the end, Mrs. Appleby had ordered a taxi and brought her home from Gilda's.

Piers flew up the stairs and into the bedroom, throwing his arms around her. Ignoring the pain as he held her close, she wet his neck with her tears. After several minutes he pulled back to look at her battered face.

"I must look a fright," she said with a shy grin.

"Nonsense! But you have an open egg on your head that's turning blue, and angry purple shadows under your eyes. I think we should call a doctor to come and check you out. You may have a concussion."

"Is that really necessary?" she asked, basking in his attentions.

"Absolutely! I'll be right back." He left as she reached out a hand.

Before he got to the phone it began to ring. His voice was muffled, but then he let out an expletive which came through the floor loud and clear. She wondered who it was.

Piers reappeared. "That was Bob from the garage. Your brake line was cut!"

# Chapter 16

Piers was back in the bedroom, sitting next to Percy, legs up on the bed.

"This is serious," he said, watching her sip hot milk brought up by Mrs. Appleby. "Has anything unusual happened recently?"

"My cousin was murdered," she whispered.

"I meant to you?" He took her hand and rubbed his thumb over her knuckles.

"I did run into some people who had been at the gallery that day," she said.

"Like who?" he asked, turning his body to face her, concern etched all over his sweet face.

"I was up in London, and I ran into the man who backed Nigel. Sir William Packett." There was no need to admit to her husband that she was stalking him.

"Packett," he repeated slowly. "Did he act strangely?"

"Not really, though he is a bit of an odd duck. Wears a monocle. Anyway, it was for the unveiling of a new picture at the Charing Gallery. He was there too, and we recognized each other."

"That's just a coincidence then," he remarked.

*Well...*

"He did lie to me," she admitted.

"Oh?"

"At first he said he hadn't met Nigel before his exhibition and did not know where he lived, but when I mentioned asking Agatha if he could have a look at Nigel's other paintings, he said he hadn't been to Hampshire in a while." She thrust out her chin and immediately regretted it. "Piers! He had just told me he didn't know where Nigel lived."

"That is peculiar. Why lie about it if he had nothing to hide?"

"Exactly. And there's something else. I bumped into Lord Banbury at the presentation of a new war memorial. He was interested in investing in one of Nigel's paintings. He took me for tea and things got a bit...awkward."

Pier's face was aghast. "Awkward how? Did he make a pass at you?"

If Percy's head and ribs didn't hurt so much, she would have laughed uncontrollably. Instead, she made a little grunt. "Are you joking? I'm not exactly movie star material."

He squeezed her hand. "You are to me."

Percy felt her lip tremble, and the skin between her eyes tightened. "Really?"

"Really." He slid across the bed to kneel facing her and took both her hands in his. "Percy, I could have lost you today."

He moved forward, pressing his forehead gently against hers, and though it hurt her goose egg like mad, she bit her lip through the pain so as not to break the rare, magical moment.

"When this project is over, I'm going to take some leave. Let's go away to Paris or somewhere."

She pulled back, her forehead throbbing. "Paris? Just you and me?"

"Yes, I've been neglecting you, and this accident has helped me realign my priorities. *You* are the most important thing in my life, Percy. I've been taking that for granted."

The tears bubbled over again but not because of the accident. She had missed her husband, felt overlooked, and the fact that he was recognizing that, was wonderful.

"I'd like that."

The doctor had arrived, looked into her eyes with a light and moved it around, asking if she felt sick. He had pressed on her ribs making her gasp and concluded that she had merely bruised them. Having administered a sleeping draft, the doctor departed after conducting a whispered conversation with Piers.

By the time Percy awoke, her husband had left for work.

She laid still, assessing her head and chest. The pain in her skull had decreased to a dull thud, but her ribs stabbed with every breath. She pushed back the covers, wincing as her tender chest objected, crossed the room to the window and pulled back the curtains. Martha Peabody was walking her beagle, and Percy had a flashback of the man with the collie. She squeezed her eyes tight, reliving the memory. She could swear it was the same build and gait as Lord Banbury.

She shook her head. What would he be doing walking his dog in Fetching? No, that was silly unless…

The phone rang and she waited for Mrs. Appleby to get it.

After answering, she heard the cook say, "She's not up yet, Mr. Pontefract."

"I am!" she shouted, regretting it almost immediately. She clutched her ribcage. Had the cook heard her? "I'm up!"

She threw a thick robe haphazardly around her shoulders and thundered down the stairs, giddy as a schoolgirl. Grabbing the phone from a wide-eyed Mrs. Appleby, whose hand was clamped over her mouth, Percy said, "Piers!"

"I was just checking on my girl. How are you feeling this morning, darling?"

"My head is much better, thank you, and I slept like a log. I didn't even hear you leave." She left out the detail about her screaming ribs.

"Percy, I've been thinking. I want you to stay around the house for the next few days. To lay low. After the doctor left, I called the police, and they came round to get a police report. Someone cut your brakes. This was no accident. They are going to investigate, but it has made me nervous for your safety. I can't help but feel it has something to do with your cousin's murder. I asked the local police to contact Chief Inspector Thompson. I think it prudent that you remain at home for the time being."

"Alright. What about the dog? Can I not even walk him?"

"Percy, you're in no physical condition to walk the dog, anyway. I'll try to get home in time to give him a run. It's just for a few days. Can you do that?"

"Of course."

"Bob is still assessing whether it's worth trying to save your old car. When you're feeling up to it, we'll go on that trip to Paris. Get away from here."

They said goodbye and she padded into the kitchen, heart heavy, mourning her beloved car.

"Oh my!" cried Mrs. Appleby, almost dropping the jug she was holding.

"What?" cried Percy.

"I thought you looked bad in the dark hall but in the light, you look like you've been in a boxing ring and lost," the cook replied.

Percy rushed back into the hall to look in the long mirror. The purple bump on her head was more swollen, distorting her face, and the black and blue bruising under her eyes had traveled even further south. She let out a yelp. She looked positively frightening. Put on a black, hooded cape and she could pass for the ghost of Christmas past. Or the grim reaper himself.

It would be easy to keep her promise to Piers, as there was no way she was going out in public looking like this.

She scooted back into the kitchen, biting back a grin. "I can see why you nearly dropped the jug. I would frighten tiny dogs and small children." She eased her aching body into a chair, and Mrs. Appleby pushed a mug of tea toward her.

"Did you hear Piers say my brakes were cut?" she asked.

"I did. Who would do that?" The cook stopped and turned slowly back. "You don't think it has anything to do with…"

Percy nodded. "I do. So does Piers. I've made someone nervous enough to try to kill me. Sleuthing is not so much fun when you are the prey." Her heart was thudding in her chest. "Piers wants me to stay home while the police carry out their investigation."

"I agree. It's not worth putting yourself in danger."

Mrs. Appleby turned back to wash up some bowls and Percy pulled the newspaper toward her. The front-page headline concerned an assassination attack against Mussolini in Italy. A bomb meant to kill him had killed seventeen bystanders. She shuddered, turning the first page and stopped dead in her tracks. Inside, was an article featuring a gorgeous mansion house she knew only too well. The dowager's country estate.

*Chiltern Park, ancestral home of the current Earl of Kent, and its contents, is to be put up for auction. All interested parties should contact Messrs. Parke and Taylor.*

She let the paper fall. That beautiful house was on the auction block? Why? What did it mean?

Her head began to thud, and she moved upstairs in search of more aspirin.

Staring into the bathroom mirror, her hideous reflection staring back, she pondered. *The dowager, the house, Nigel, the paintings. Her brakes. Was there a connection?*

The following day, Percy looked even worse, like she had been hit by a red London bus. The swelling on her head had gone down a little, but the bruises were parading proudly like peacocks. For once she was grateful the boys were at school.

They had received word early that morning that her cherished car was not worth repairing. She would need to purchase a new one. Percy received the news as one might on learning of the passing of a treasured pet. Piers pointed out that at least it was the car that was broken beyond repair and not Percy.

Piers had continued his tender ministrations, and she was secretly grateful that the silver lining of such a terrible ordeal was the increased attention from her husband. She entertained herself by making plans about what they would do together in Paris.

Kissing her on the forehead as he brought her a tray for breakfast, Piers promised not to be late home. After he left, Percy took a bite of the delicious toast and homemade marmalade as she picked up the folded newspaper.

The first headline grabbed her attention.

*'Art World Turned Upside Down As Police Announce Infiltration Of Master Forger's Work'*

Could this be about Nigel? Chief Inspector Thompson had not contacted her since leaving him the fake Vermeer. But then again, she supposed she was just another suspect in her cousin's murder. He did not owe her any involvement.

Toast forgotten, Percy studied the story.

*"Art authorities are reeling this morning from a police statement that an unknown artist has been flooding the market with forgeries through an intermediary for private sale. Using a hitherto unknown process, the artist was able to perfect the aging of the paint in order to fool some of the biggest names in art authentication.*

*Though the scale of the enterprise is not yet known, it appears that an elaborate scam was created that played on ego and vanity to successfully defraud collectors. Only*

124

*paintings that were no longer on public display appear to have been reproduced.*

*If you suspect that a recently acquired, private sale painting is such a forgery, you are encouraged to call Scotland Yard immediately."*

Percy thought back to the painting she had discovered. An unsuspecting public would easily succumb to such a hoax if the sale were presented in the right light. A swindle that stroked the ego of the wealthy. She imagined a trusted "expert" could convince art collectors that the "authenticated" painting had been sold in secret by owners who were in sudden need of cash, and that in order to preserve the privacy of the owner, the sale needed to be undertaken to only the most *discreet* of clients—of which there were several, bidding on the painting.

The ringing of the doorbell interrupted her musings.

"Where *is* she?" The all-too-familiar, dreadful honking of her mother floated through the floor of her bedroom, and Percy had to reject an impulse to hide under the covers.

Pounding footsteps on the stairs heralded Mrs. Crabtree's ascent, and Percy held her breath, gripping the coverlet for courage.

"Let me look at you!" cried her mother, heading straight for the curtains to pull them further back. Percy squinted in the sunlight. Her mother spun on her heels and gasped.

"Hideous!" Clearly, her mother needed coaching on compassion and care of the sick and needy. "Could you have any permanent damage?"

"It is mostly bumps and bruises," Percy replied. "The doctor thinks my face should be cleared up in ten days."

"Ten days! You would do well to stay home until you are completely healed, Persephone. I—we have a reputation to uphold. We can't have you looking like you lost a bar brawl."

A crowd of cutting retorts made their way to Percy's brain, but she merely said, "I don't feel up to going out."

Her mother was standing at the foot of the bed, clutching her handbag. "Thank heavens for that! Is anything broken?"

*My spirits.* "I was lucky. Apart from the blow to the head and bruised ribs, I am all in one piece."

"Well, that *is* fortunate." Mrs. Crabtree pulled a chair to the side of the bed. "What about your car?"

Percy was still quite emotional about the little car's demise and fought to gain her composure. "Dead," she responded. "Unrepairable." She did not add that it was impounded by the police once Piers reported that the brake line had been cut.

Mrs. Crabtree leaned forward to examine Percy's face, much as the art dealer had examined the fake Vermeer. "Shocking!" she tutted. "How could this happen? Piers needs to maintain your vehicles better."

It wasn't worth the fight to defend her husband against the charges of neglect, as her mother would not be persuaded otherwise, and Percy did not have the energy to oppose her mother today.

After offering unsolicited advice on which ointments to apply in order to hasten the healing process, Mrs. Crabtree launched into an update on her opposition to the proposed road. *Uggh!* Percy closed her eyes hoping her mother would attribute her lack of attention to the accident.

# Chapter 17

On the fourth day of recuperation, Percy received a somewhat unexpected visit from the handsome Chief Inspector Thompson. Recognizing his voice rumbling through the floorboards, her courage flagged as she heard Mrs. Appleby show him into the front sitting room. The bruises under her eyes were now a dull shade of yellow, and the gash on her head scabbed and ugly. Piers had mentioned the inspector's intent to visit in passing, but she hadn't really thought he would make the trek out to the country.

She hopped out of bed and immediately regretted it as the room spun and she clutched the bed post. Feeling her way to the dressing table, she sunk onto the padded bench and recoiled at her image. She could earn a fortune at a *World's Strangest Creatures* carnival.

Her hair had taken advantage of her convalescence and had the distinct air of electric shock. She smashed it with her hands, but it bounced back like a sheep's fleece. Opening a drawer for inspiration, she laid eyes on a silk scarf. *Perfect!* Placing it over her head, she rolled the ends and brought them up to her crown, tying them with a double knot. It wasn't ideal, but it did cover her wild and frenzied, untamable mop.

Not one for heavy makeup, she usually made do with a quick swipe of lipstick and an occasional foray into tricky mascara. But today she wished she had sent out for some greasepaint to disguise the bruising, or at least some face powder. Her mother's words rang in her head. *Hideous.* Oh, well! She *had* gone through a near death experience, after all.

Rather than reveal the utilitarian dressing gown she usually wore, Percy went to the wardrobe and pulled out a silky wrap Piers had bought on one of his longer trips. It was vermillion with large, white flowers splashed across it which clashed with her bruises. She had gained weight since the purchase and had to stretch the thin fabric across her middle, wrestling the two sides together by tying the belt tightly across her stomach. She glanced at her comfortable men's slippers and grimaced. She had no dainty, silk pair with ostrich feathers to match the femininity of the peignoir. She hastily pulled off her homemade woolen socks and slid her extra-large feet into the ugly house shoes.

"Mrs. Pontefract!" sang Mrs. Appleby in her poshest voice. "The chief inspector is here to see you."

Taking it slow, Percy left her room, and, gripping the banister tightly, made her way cautiously down the stairs.

At the sight of Mrs. Appleby's bulging eyes, Percy regretted her choice of outfit. "Do I look awful?"

Mrs. Appleby pursed her lips, and Percy could not tell if she was really biting back laughter. "I've just never seen you wearing a fancy wrap," she said, her voice wobbly. "Or a scarf over your hair, for that matter."

"Should I go back and change?" Percy was fearful of looking ridiculous in front of the inspector.

"No, you look fine. You shouldn't keep the chief inspector waiting."

Though Percy wanted to run back up the stairs and send Mrs. Appleby to inform the inspector that she was not feeling up to a visit, the cook was right; she had already kept him waiting long enough and he had come quite a long way to see her. She pulled the front of the wrap tighter and made for the sitting room door.

"Good morning, Chief Inspector."

He had been standing at the window, gazing at the sheep farm on the other side of the road. When he turned, his face froze in shock.

The peignoir had been the wrong choice. She sagged.

"Mrs. Pontefract!" he began, his rich voice full of the concern that had been lacking in her own mother's tone. "I did not appreciate the extent of your injuries."

Her hand went to her face. "I'm doing much better, actually." She pointed to a chair. "Please, sit down."

His eyes were drawn to her like some macabre curiosity in a museum, and she squirmed under his empathetic scrutiny. After a moment, he seemed to realize that such close examination was rude and dropped his eyes to the floor while searching in his pocket for a notebook. She looked down to see the peignoir gaping at the front, exposing her modest, flannel nightdress. She pulled at it again, holding the fabric together with her fist.

"I have some questions about your accident," began the inspector. "I have talked to the garage owner and seen the brake line myself. There is no question that the line was cut with a sharp knife." He looked up, earnestness radiating from his warm, brown eyes. "Can you think of any reason someone might do this to you? You're very lucky you weren't killed. That was obviously the intent."

She had deliberately spent little time reflecting on the wider issues surrounding her accident and gulped down a lump.

But it was time to put her cards on the table.

"I've tried not to think about it," she admitted, fiddling with the silky belt. "But I may have ruffled a few feathers." She told him of her various trips to London to meet up with Sir William, Lord Banbury and Syd, though she begged him not to involve the waiter unless it was absolutely necessary. She also told him of her visit to Lady Quinn.

The chief inspector shook his head with raised brows. "My, my, Mrs. Pontefract. You *have* been busy." He became serious. "Any one of these people could have arranged for your accident if they felt you were a threat."

Percy dropped her head. "I should have been more careful."

129

"The benefit is that you have succeeded in making someone very nervous, which opens up further avenues of investigation." He scribbled something in the notebook. "Do you have the note that fell from the earl's pocket? I should like to take it for analysis."

She bit her lip. Was it still in her handbag? She should be more organized if she was going to be a detect—The thought died even as it germinated. Someone had tried to kill her. She was going to find a safer hobby.

"If you will excuse me for a moment, I shall try to find it." Her limbs cracked and her ribs complained as she went into the hall and dug into her bag. As she did so, she caught a glimpse of herself in the mirror and reared back. She was a right sight.

Rummaging with her fingers, the dog barked at something in the back garden, reminding her of the stranger walking their dog away from the house. If they had come into the driveway to mess with the car, wouldn't Apollo have alerted her? As she pondered the question, she laid hold of the note and took it into the sitting room.

"I did see an unfamiliar figure walking a dog right before I had my accident," she told the inspector. "He was walking away from my house. I didn't give it much thought at the time, but now…"

"Could you identify him?"

"No, he had his back to me, wearing a large coat and a hat. And as you said, any one of these people could have hired someone to cut my brakes."

A sudden chill that nothing could warm, ambushed her. She shivered.

The chief inspector examined the note. "It does look like the same hand wrote both notes, though block capitals are much harder to scientifically process. I'll give it to the professionals to look at."

"I saw the headline in the paper today about the art forgeries. The unknown artist is Nigel, isn't it? Do you think that is the key to his death?"

Percy could see the chief inspector calculating what he should share with her.

"Ego and pride are twin vices that are powerful forces. Those in the art world are particularly prone to these characteristics. Any agent who sold a piece that proves to be a forgery will be reluctant to come forward since credibility is the key to their fortune. Any art dealer found to be the vehicle for pushing a fake picture into the world will lose their income, become a pariah.

"Likewise, those who have spent incredible amounts of money on a painting that has been certified by one of these dealers, who now fear they have been duped, will be loathed to admit it and will likely keep mum.

"Most of these types of sales are considered 'black market' purchases and are completed under the table leaving no money trail. The thrill of purchasing something rare, in secret, is part of the appeal. I suppose it gives the owner a sort of power, knowing they have something that would make their friends green with envy. These factors make this an incredibly difficult crime to solve. No one involved wants to get egg on their faces."

He closed the leather cover of his notebook. "But yes. With your valuable evidence I think it is safe to say that Mr. Fotherington was the forger, and, an as yet unknown accomplice was the seller."

"That means over one hundred people have a motive to kill Nigel," she stated.

"That's about the sum of it, yes." The chief inspector drew a hand across his forehead. "Did you see the news about the auction of Lord Kent's country home, Chiltern Park?"

"I did, as a matter of fact," said Percy. "Could there be a connection, do you think?" Her fist was cramping, and she released her death hold on the peignoir.

"The timing is interesting, but I have nothing more to go on than that," he admitted.

"The dowager invited me for tea. I forgot to mention it."

"Oh?"

"It's a beautiful estate. Did you know the dowager is a Romanov?"

The expression on the inspector's face showed that he did not.

"Her mother met and married her Russian father years before a whisper of a revolution was considered. I believe the two families were close until the tragedy."

The chief inspector leaned back in the armchair. "One of the things I really love about my job is the way a case has so many unexpected twists and turns. Life *is* stranger than fiction. It's better than going to watch a film."

"I can see that," Percy agreed. "I've even felt the thrill of it myself, but now, I confess, I'm scared."

"Well, I will be posting plain clothes policeman outside your house day and night. I brought them with me, as a matter of fact. Unfortunately, the saboteur will know by now that you have survived."

Percy felt her blood run cold, and it must have shown on her face. The inspector lifted an assuring hand. "I have my best men on the job, Mrs. Pontefract. No one will know they are here— except your household, of course. I feel quite confident in your safety. Your nasty accident is motivation to solve the case quickly and has given me some leverage. I have requested permission to investigate the finances of all the people at the gallery that day. I think it will reveal the answers we need."

# Chapter 18

"He seems like a nice man," said Mrs. Appleby after Percy had seen him to the door. "Not quite what I expect in a police inspector, somehow."

"He *is* nice, but my conversation with him has left me feeling nervous. He suggested that whoever intended to kill me will no doubt try to finish the job."

"With these bobbies hanging around the house posing as gardeners and handymen, I don't think that's likely," replied the cook, picking up another piece of silver and dabbing it with polish. "They introduced themselves and I made them a cup of tea."

Percy pulled off the scarf releasing her disorderly mane. "Piers says he is going to take me away to Paris. I wish we could leave right away."

Mrs. Appleby stopped polishing, and a dreamy look wandered around her features. "Paris. I've never been to Paris. It looks lovely."

"I've never been either, but right now its appeal is more in the fact that it is not here."

"How about we go over your case notes?" Mrs. Appleby suggested. "Keep your mind off the other thing."

"It's those notes and poking my nose in that have landed me in this position, Mrs. A. I want to wash my hands of the whole thing."

"You don't mind if I have a look, do you?" The cook laid the small tin of polish and the dirty duster aside and pushed herself up from the chair. Before approaching the drawer, she went to the larder and came back with a decent portion of apple pie, then pushed a jug of cold custard forward with a spoon. Percy's resistance was at an all-time low, and she dug into the dessert with gusto. Once she was engaged, Mrs. Appleby pulled out the infamous notebook and began looking through its pages.

"Hmmm," she said with a nod. Percy did not rise to the bait. "Oooh," the cook continued. "Well, well." Mrs. Appleby continued page after page, annotating her reading with comments that Percy ignored.

"It won't work," Percy told the cook as she scraped the bowl for the last vestiges of the custard.

"I don't know what you mean," Mrs. Appleby declared.

"Of course you do! You think if you make me curious enough, I will want to dive back into the investigation, but you are wrong, Mrs. A. I have the boys to think about."

"Guilty," replied the cook with a face just like the dog's when he was caught doing something naughty.

The doorbell rang.

"I'll get it," said Mrs. Appleby. "Are we expecting anyone?"

"Not now the inspector has left."

From the safety of the kitchen, Percy could hear the plain clothes policeman, vetting their visitor with her cook.

"Oh, m'lady," said Mrs. Appleby in that reverential tone she used around the gentry. "Please come in."

"She's alright, then?" asked the policeman.

"Oh, yes." Percy could picture Mrs. Appleby bowing and scraping in the hall.

"I am known to Mrs. Pontefract," drawled the dowager in her husky voice.

Percy sat up. *What was* she *doing here?* Percy looked down at the old, flannel nightgown and mismatched silk peignoir.

"It's quite alright officer," continued Mrs. Appleby. "I'll show you to the sitting room."

Percy heard the front door close and waited for the cook to come back before she rushed upstairs to change out of her plain nightie.

Mrs. Appleby returned to the kitchen, eyes wide as plates. "It's that Romanov princess," she hissed.

"I know!" replied Percy in a strangled whisper. "Can you make us some more tea? I need to change." Percy scurried down the hall, grabbing the newel post as her head spun. Stopping, she took a couple of deep breaths before slowly taking the stairs one step at a time.

In her room she threw off the silky robe and ripped off the sensible nightdress. Glancing in the mirror she saw her hair, wild as a South American jungle and the yellow bruises on her face.

She inhaled a deep breath of resignation.

Grabbing a gray skirt, and a blouse whose colors vaguely matched the headscarf, she slipped them on. Then clutching handfuls of hair, she maneuvered the scarf over the rampant curls. Sitting briefly in front of her dressing table, she tied the two ends tightly on the top. Again.

*There!*

She still looked like a spirit returned from the dead, but at least she was now a well-dressed phantom.

Taking a moment to catch her breath and willing her head to stop whirling, she descended the stairs. The dizziness was really bad today and was upsetting her stomach. She clutched her middle with a hand in an effort to soothe away the nausea. *No luck.*

Plastering a smile on her face, she opened the door to the sitting room. The dowager was wearing a decidedly more British outfit today: a dark, wool coat and ankle-length woolen skirt. Several animals had sacrificed their lives for her hat. Her presence was too big for the small room.

"I'm so sorry to keep you waiting," Percy blurted out as the dowager gasped, a hand to her chest. Percy touched her face. "I look awful, I know. I don't own any face powder."

The dowager cleared her throat. "I heard from your Aunt Agatha that you had been in an accident. Since I was in the neighborhood, I thought it only right to offer my

135

condolences." Her jaw rolled like a cow chewing the cud as she spoke.

"Agatha is my second cousin," she began to remind her. "She's actually my mother's cousin. Never mind. It gets complicated."

Mrs. Appleby entered with a bulging tray of tea and cake, relieving Percy of the need to explain more.

"Tea?" Percy asked.

"Thank you," said the dowager. "Two sugars."

Percy concentrated on not spilling the tea as every muscle in her arm complained about the weight of the pot. She plopped two sugars in and placed a tiny silver spoon on the saucer before handing it to the dowager.

She began to pour herself a cup but felt her stomach roll. However, it would be rude to let the dowager drink alone, so she continued to fill the cup to further the pretense that she was going to drink. She popped a sugar cube in and stirred.

"It was a car accident, I understand," the dowager began, brows raised in invitation.

Percy had no intention of divulging that her car had been sabotaged. At this point she didn't really know who to trust, and besides, Piers had asked her to keep it all confidential.

"Yes, silly really. I swerved to miss a deer." That much was true. "I over-corrected the steering wheel and crashed off the road and down an embankment."

The dowager's steely eyes narrowed. "My dear, you could have been killed."

"I-I know," Percy stuttered. "It was terrifying."

"I am so glad to see that you survived." The older woman laid heavy emphasis on the 'so'. "But I can see that you are badly hurt. Shouldn't you be in a hospital?"

Percy explained that her injuries looked worse than they were.

After an awkward pause, Percy filled the silence with talk about her boys. She really wanted to ask about the sale

136

of the dowager's home but thought it would be too intrusive.

"Do you have a picture of your children?" asked the dowager after Percy had chattered non-stop for five minutes.

"Oh, yes. Hang on a jiffy." Percy leapt out of the chair, regretting it immediately, and lunged for the door. Leaning against the wall in the hall, she waited for her equilibrium to return then hurried into the living room. She grabbed a recent picture of the boys in a silver frame and hastened back to the sitting room.

Handing the photograph to the dowager countess, the great lady hummed approval. "What strong-looking boys."

"They are full of vigor and vim," Percy agreed. "But they are at boarding school, and I miss them terribly."

"Nurses and nannies reared my children," said the dowager. "It was the way we did it back then. I saw them for about fifteen minutes a day most of the time. It suited me."

Percy looked down so that the horror she felt would not be exposed across her battered features.

When she finally looked up, the dowager was casting a critical eye on Percy's full cup, and she picked it up, but the speed with which she had fetched the picture had increased her light-headedness and her stomach was staging a revolt that even tea could not conquer. She pretended to take a sip and kept the cup raised to her chest.

"Do have some cake, Countess."

"I do not eat cake before four o'clock," she explained, the wrinkles on her cheeks stiff. "It does not agree with me. Alas, as we age our digestion becomes our enemy."

The talk turned to the weather and other mundane topics, and then the dowager placed her cane firmly on the ground and hoisted herself up.

"I am glad to see that you are recovering," she said as she made to leave.

Percy intercepted the dowager so that she could open the door and lead the auspicious woman into the vestibule.

"It was so kind of you to visit." Percy held the front door wide and noticed a long, sleek car in her driveway. A driver in full uniform was leaning against the gleaming vehicle, but upon seeing the dowager, he stood up, straight as a pin.

"Give my regards to your husband," said the dowager as she turned to approach the vehicle.

Percy watched as the driver helped the old lady in, drove out of the driveway and onto the country road. She scratched her head.

Returning to the sitting room she tried to lift the tray, but her arms hurt too much. "Mrs. Appleby!"

When the cook appeared, Percy explained the problem and Mrs. Appleby grabbed the tray. "Tch! You didn't touch your tea."

"My poor head is making my tummy feel awful. I couldn't face it," Percy explained.

"Never mind. I'll give it to the dog. Apollo loves a good cuppa."

Percy followed her cook into the kitchen then decided she needed to rest.

"No problem, Mrs. Pontefract. I'll be getting dinner ready. Go and take a nice nap."

Piers was pulling her gently up the iron stairs of the Eiffel tower, giggling, when he stretched open his mouth and screamed. A blood-curdling screech.

Percy's eyes snapped open.

Momentarily confused that it was full daylight, the scream came again, coming closer. She sat bolt upright, regretting it immediately as the near constant wooziness assailed her. Closing her eyes, she jumped when Mrs. Appleby slammed into the room.

"A squirrel drank your tea. It's dead!"

# Chapter 19

Percy's heart was already racing from being jerked awake so violently, but Mrs. Appleby's words had it galloping even faster.

"I'm confused," Percy began, trying to get her scattered emotions in some sort of order. "A squirrel?"

Face blanched, Mrs. Appleby flapped her arms. "I took the tea and like I said, I thought the dog might like it, so I put it in his bowl. He was off somewhere chasing rabbits, and a squirrel must have seen the tea and come for a drink. I went out to flick a tablecloth of crumbs and found the squirrel stiff as a board next to the bowl. The first thing I did was throw the rest of the tea down the drain so the dog didn't drink it."

"You think there was something in my tea?" asked Percy, trying to run a hand through her hair but getting stuck in all the tangles.

Mrs. Appleby's features were frozen in fear. "I do."

Lifting back the covers, Percy swung her legs around and sat on the edge of the bed, her mind still as knotted as her hair.

"But only you and I touched the tea—" Percy stopped short. "The dowager."

She locked eyes with Mrs. Appleby. "I went to get a picture of the boys. She must have put something in my cup while I was gone. We can have the chief inspector send it to a lab. Have you told the undercover policemen?"

The cook wailed. "No! I forgot all about them! And worse, I washed up the cup ages ago and the rest of your tea is down the drain and in the sewer." She slammed a hand to her chest, her lip trembling. "It could have been you."

The same ugly thought had been hovering around the edges of Percy's brain, but Mrs. Appleby had placed it front and center. Fear slid under her skin like a specter taking up residence.

"And everyone would have put my death down to some internal injury from the accident," she murmured. "I need to call the chief inspector. Now!" She ran to the top of the stairs, grabbing the newel to steady herself, then hobbled down the stairs as fast as she could.

"Scotland Yard," she barked into the line as soon as the telephone exchange answered.

When she finally got through to Chief Inspector Thompson, the terror had transformed to fiery anger. How dare the woman use an invitation to tea to try to *murder* her!

"Thompson."

"Chief Inspector!" She could sense the hysteria in her voice.

"Mrs. Pontefract. Is everything alright?"

"No! Everything is *not* alright!" She relayed everything that had happened after he left her house.

"You no longer have the tea? That is a shame," he said with a sigh. "What about the squirrel?"

Mrs. Appleby was standing by her in the hall with a face like a wet Wednesday. "Where is the squirrel?" Percy demanded.

The cook's mournful eyes widened. "In the bin. I'll get it." She hurried out to the back patio.

"We have the squirrel!" declared Percy, as triumphant as if she were declaring herself the winner of the race to swim the Channel. Fury was making her uncharacteristically bold.

"Give it to one of my men and they can rush it to the police lab."

"Will do!" she replied.

"Speaking of my men, how did the dowager get past them?"

"They did intercept her but Mrs. Appleby vouched for the old lady. She is a dowager countess, after all."

A sound of frustration made its way down the line. "Given the circumstances, you should not trust anyone, Mrs. Pontefract. I shall be having a word with my officers." There was a short pause. "Remember the Earl of Kent's home is on the auction block?" the inspector asked her.

"How could I forget?" she retorted. "I wanted to ask her about it but thought it would be rude. Ha! Rude!"

She could hear the chief inspector clear his throat, or was he laughing at her righteous indignation? She didn't care.

"Well, when I returned to my office, I found a financial report on my desk showing that the family has been underwater for some time. The documents also held the record of an undisclosed, hefty investment made last year. I would place good money on a wager that they hoped this investment would save their bacon."

"Nigel's forgeries," whispered Percy.

"My thoughts exactly," said the inspector. "It would certainly explain why she came all the way to London for his art exhibition when she didn't even like modern art. The family must have tried to sell the painting to realize the funds, only to be told they had been duped. I imagine the daring dowager made it her sole objective in life to root out the person responsible and make them pay. I wouldn't be surprised if she considered the invitation arriving like that, a sign. Killing the man responsible for their ultimate financial downfall must have felt like poetic justice."

"It must have been the dowager who tampered with my car—well, not she herself, but an employee of hers. She *was* rather odd when we were talking about my accident." Percy thought back on the heavy emphasis the dowager had laid on how lucky she had been.

"When she heard you survived, she came to finish off the job," remarked the chief inspector.

"I would have died in my sleep, and everyone would have attributed it to the bash on my head. I've heard of people having brain bleeds after bad accidents."

"You are a *very* lucky woman," exclaimed the inspector. "Twice over!"

"What are we going to do?" demanded Percy, her fist clenched.

"We?"

"That woman has tried to kill me twice. I want to see her arrested," cried Percy.

"Woah! We have no actual evidence that it *was* the tea since your cook tipped it away. The squirrel could just have been old and died of natural causes. Until the lab examines the rodent, I have no reasonable grounds on which to arrest the countess. And if she did try to poison you, the dowager is unlikely to have kept the poison. She probably threw it out of the window somewhere between your house and hers. She's a cunning old girl."

"How long will the tests take?" Percy demanded with Dutch courage borne of the boiling anger.

"A couple of days."

"That's too long!" said Percy. "She could leave the country by then." She bit her nails.

"I must tread carefully given that the dowager is a member of the aristocracy," explained the chief inspector. "When the lab results are conclusive, and *if* they show that the squirrel was, in fact, poisoned, then I will have means and opportunity. I assume the motive is that she thought you were close to discovering that it was she who killed your cousin. Only after conclusive results from the lab can I arrest her. It will make headlines, Mrs. Pontefract. I can't afford to make any mistakes."

"There's nothing we can do before that?" Percy was becoming hysterical. "Can't you search the property for the painting?"

"The *alleged* painting. We have no proof that is what actually happened. At this point it is little more than a theory. I can't just barge into the estate and start looking for something I don't even know is there."

"What about the auction? I understand it is being held at the estate tomorrow." She had bitten her nails so much that one of her fingers was beginning to bleed. She searched her pockets for a handkerchief.

"Now, now Mrs. Pontefract. This isn't one of those adventure films. We need to have patience and do things in the proper way."

"You'll let me know as soon as you get the lab results?" she pushed.

"Yes," he promised.

"Will you at least question her?"

There was a pause. "I don't want to tip my hand. I'd rather go straight for an arrest if the results show poisoning."

Irritation was crawling over Percy like a nest of ants. "Of course. Thank you, Inspector."

She placed the phone back in its cradle.

*He* may be bound by procedure, but she wasn't! Her mind was falling over itself making plans.

When Percy and Mrs. Appleby pulled up to Chiltern Park, there were so many cars the gardener was directing people where to park. Mrs. Appleby, who had come under duress, was nonetheless impressed by the home.

Percy had sent Mrs. Appleby to the chemist's shop to buy some face powder the minute she had ended her conversation with the chief inspector, and discussed her ambitious plans over dinner, plans that included the cook. Mrs. Appleby was doubtful.

One of the plain clothes policemen who had been guarding the house took the squirrel and conveyed it to the chief inspector. Hampered by the fact it would take so long, and still stinging with indignation, Percy had determined to attend the auction the next day. The house would be open to the public for the auction and would give her the freedom she needed to poke around.

She and Mrs. Appleby joined the throng entering the dramatic entrance. Seats had been set up in the large foyer, and auctioneers were handing out bidding paddles. She grabbed a brochure, maneuvered past them, and found two seats near the back.

Looking around, Percy was sure that a lot of the people in attendance were just being nosy. It was the kind of thing her mother would do. Mrs. Appleby was gripping the handles of her handbag as though they were a life buoy. Percy laid a reassuring hand on her cook's arm.

"The family probably aren't even here," she said. "I can't imagine they would want to witness the sale of the house and contents they hold so dear. We are perfectly safe today."

"If you say so," murmured the cook.

The room was filled to capacity within five minutes, and people were forced to stand up on the sides. A formal gentleman came to a podium labeled "*Crystals of London*" and cleared his throat loudly. The room fell silent.

"Remember," whispered Percy urgently. "Whatever you do, don't lift a hand to wipe your nose or rub your eye or even wink. I know we don't have a paddle, but I'm not sure how these things work, and I would hate to be on the hook for this place."

Mrs. Appleby's grip on her handbag became even tighter.

The catalogue showed that many items were to be auctioned off before the finale of the house itself. As soon as the bidding began on the smaller pieces, Percy made her move. Mrs. Appleby grabbed her arm in a vice grip.

"Be careful, Mrs. Pontefract."

"Will do," Percy assured her.

She had a plan.

Following the hallway she had taken with the ponderous butler, she came to a fork. She wanted to find the attics—the part used for storage, not where the servants lived. The sale brochure had come with a convenient map of the house for prospective buyers, and she withdrew it from her pocket. Hidden in the paneling facing her was a door to the servant's quarters. She pushed a few panels before finding the correct one and found herself in a plain stairwell that went up and down.

Climbing the stone stairs, she came to a landing. Referring to the map once again, she learned that the door to the right was for the female staff and the door straight ahead was for males. The door on the left was labeled "storage" on the map. Trying that one, she was disappointed to find it locked.

*Drat!*

A noise from Percy's left showed a woman, who could only be a housekeeper, at the end of the hallway for female servants, headed straight toward her. Panicked, Percy grabbed the first handle she could and stepped into a dark broom cupboard. She pulled the door closed.

The jingle and scraping of keys indicated that the housekeeper had locked the female door behind her, but instead of leaving, Percy heard another scraping of keys. She opened the cupboard door a fraction and saw the woman opening the door to the storage corridor. Entering, the woman in black left the door ajar, indicating that her stay would be of short duration.

Heart in her throat, Percy waited for her footsteps to dim, then flashed from the cupboard and into the corridor praying there would be somewhere to hide. If not, she had an excuse for her presence—she was looking for the lavatories.

Narrow, dusty and dark, the hallway was home to various doors. She opened the first to hide herself and entered a space with a dirty dormer window, full of decrepit cradles and mothy rocking horses. The sound of footsteps returning had her looking around the room for cover. Seeing a large doll's house, she ducked down behind it.

*How are you going to get out?* She would cross that bridge when she came to it.

Her nose began to tickle. She was going to sneeze because of all the dust. Pulling out a large handkerchief, she slammed it against her nose, body tense as the biological reaction came to a head. Trying to absorb the energy and the noise internally, she stiffened even more. She managed to suffocate the sneeze until it became little more than a burp, but she suffered the absorption of the energy in other areas of her body. Now she *really* needed the lavatory.

The housekeeper's crisp footsteps passed by and the sound of the keys turning in the lock assured Percy that she was safe. Emerging from behind the doll's house, she looked around the room. No painting.

Re-entering the hallway, Percy tried the next door. This room was packed with old chairs, springs poking through faded fabric, and missing legs. A quick look around the room was unproductive.

After two more rooms with the same result, she came to the last door. This room was brimming with old knickknacks. Centuries of refuse and souvenirs lay in a state of genteel decay. She wandered around the room, losing heart. Where could she go next if this proved to be another dead end?

A once-glorious wardrobe with an inlaid border of walnut stood, its door hanging off like a drunken sailor. She squeezed through tea chests and old dressers but felt her spirits fall when she found the inside of the wardrobe to be empty. The fire in her belly that had been fueled by anger that the dowager had the temerity to try to knock her off was waning. She was locked in a corridor of a home she did not own and had found nothing of worth to prove her case. She slid down the side of the wardrobe in despair. *How was she going to get out of here?* A quick glance at her watch showed that she had already been gone for thirty-five minutes. Mrs. Appleby would be doing her crust.

Shuffling to get more comfortable, Percy's arm hit something. Upon inspection she saw that it was a blank canvas. It was the first item that had held any hope. But a blank canvas was of little use. She hung her head.

*Wait a minute.*

Everything in the attics was covered in a thick layer of dust. She opened her eyes and looked at the canvas again. It was spotless. Her heart began to jiggle with excitement. She picked up the frame and turned it over, searching. The dirty dormer obscured the light, and she stood and took the frame close to the glass. There, in pencil, on the wooden frame, was a number. *110.*

One of the corners was loose, and she wiggled a finger under the stiff, blank cloth stretched over the wood. Her heart began to quiver as her eyes caught a flash of color. The white cloth was covering something! A seed of optimism took root. Taking the coarse material in her fingers, Percy yanked hard and gasped.

Beneath her gaze was *The Milk Maid* by Botticelli.

# Chapter 20

Percy stared at the impossibly beautiful painting. Nigel was truly gifted.

Footsteps sounded, and she quickly stretched the plain, white canvas back over the breathtaking painting beneath, crouching behind the wardrobe, terrified of discovery.

"Mrs. Pontefract!" called a muffled male voice. "This is Sergeant Twister of the Ashford police, and I am here to arrest you on the charge of trespassing."

A pit opened in her stomach. *What was happening?*

"You were seen entering this corridor twenty minutes ago, and I am here to take you into custody and conduct you to the station. I have no desire to waste valuable police time searching every nook and cranny. I am asking you to surrender."

She was literally a rabbit in a trap.

Getting to her feet, Percy straightened her skirt and slunk out into the corridor. What would Piers say? *Crickey!* What would her *mother* say? If she had possessed a tail, it would now be between her legs.

The stern sergeant's eyes brightened as she emerged. "Very sensible, madam." He turned to the housekeeper. "I've got it from here." The housekeeper made her way back down the corridor as the policeman took Percy's hands and placed them behind her back. The cold steel of the handcuffs chilled her further and the dizziness returned, but this time it had nothing to do with her concussion.

"I am arresting you on the charge of trespassing and burglary—"

"Hold on!" cried Percy. "I haven't taken a thing!"

The housekeeper turned her head to the side as she walked, a sneer of contentment on her face.

"—and burglary," continued the policeman in a rather loud voice. "It is my duty to transport you to the police station where you will be officially charged and a statement taken."

Percy's eyes began to sting. "B-but I-I can't…"

"It's alright, Mrs. Pontefract," he said lowering his voice. "I'm here at the behest of Chief Inspector Thompson. Just play along."

Percy's eyes snapped to his as her knees went weak with relief. The constable gave her a sly wink.

"I just got lost!" Percy wailed, playing her part. "I was trying to find the lavatory."

Giving the housekeeper plenty of time to be out of earshot, the policeman said, "Chief Inspector Thompson was sure you would try to find the painting you both believe is here and asked me to follow you. Which I did, all the way up to these attics."

*Bless him!*

"Just how did you think you were going to get out of here?" he asked with a chuckle.

"I hadn't thought that far ahead," Percy admitted.

"Well, when I saw you sneak into the hall and then observed the housekeeper lock you in, I knew something had to be done. So, I gave you time to have a poke around and then told the housekeeper that I was here because someone had reported an intruder."

"I am ever so grateful," she said, feeling her face heat up. "It was a conundrum to be sure."

"Did you find anything?" he asked.

"Follow me, Sergeant," she said, leading him back to the last room. She motioned with her shoulder because her hands were still locked behind her back. "Is there any way you can take these off?"

"Best not," he said. "Just in case someone comes."

He squatted down by the blank canvas with a confused expression.

"Peel back the white upper layer, Sergeant."

"Oh!" he exclaimed as he did. "What a beauty!"

150

"Isn't it? Even though my cousin was a crook, I can't help but admire his abilities." The handcuffs were uncomfortable and forced her to hold her bag with both hands behind her. She needed to move things along. "Now, how are we going to get it out?"

"I'll reattach the outer canvas and say it is evidence because you were going to steal it."

"Oh, very good."

He stretched the white material back over the painting and held it where the blank canvas was loose so that a casual observer would not notice. Standing, the painting secure in his grip, he announced, "Now, Mrs. Pontefract, you will have to summon any acting skills you possess until I get you safely in the police car."

"But my cook, Mrs. Appleby, is in the auction room."

"You'll need to pretend this is all real if we are going to get you and the painting out of here successfully. Can you do that?"

Percy bit her bottom lip. "If I must."

The officer frogmarched her out of the narrow corridor and into the main hallway of the servant's quarters, past two startled parlor maids, and down the stairs. Another, much younger policeman, was at the bottom of the staircase.

"We need to tell this lady's cook that she needs to accompany us, Bert. She's in the auction room."

"Yes, sir," said the baby-faced constable. "Can you give me a description?"

Percy described Mrs. Appleby down to her purple rinse and the heirloom brooch on her coat collar, and the three of them walked through the hidden panel door and into the main area of the house. Percy hung her head while they waited for the constable to retrieve the cook. Even though it was all a sham, she would die if she saw anyone she knew.

On seeing Percy handcuffed like a common criminal, Mrs. Appleby almost fainted and had to brace herself against the wall. "Oh, my heavens!"

The constable offered her his arm, but not an explanation.

"I knew this was a hare-brained idea," Mrs. Appleby whispered as they all walked out the front entrance of Chiltern Park, "but I never imagined you would go and get yourself arrested! What will your mother have to say about *this*?"

Percy regretted that she could offer no words of reassurance, but knew it was vital to keep up the ruse, and her cook's reaction only gave credence to the arrest as several eyes followed them to the entrance.

The constable held the rear door of the car open and helped Percy in, hands still behind her back. Then he helped the moaning Mrs. Appleby slide in beside Percy.

"I hope no one I know sees me," Mrs. Appleby exclaimed, echoing Percy's own sentiments. "I'll never live it down."

"Thank you, Constable," said the officer who had arrested her. "Can you get back to the station by yourself?"

"I've got my bicycle, thank you, sir," he explained and patted the top of the car.

The police vehicle pulled away, and Mrs. Appleby began a remorseful rant that she had been unsuccessful in convincing Percy not to do something so reckless.

The arresting officer began to chuckle.

Brow knitted, Mrs. Appleby tipped her head toward the bobby as if he were a lunatic, which made Percy burst out laughing.

Rearranging her shoulders, the poor cook cried, "I don't know what's going on here, but I demand that someone tell me, immediately!"

Chief Inspector Thompson was waiting for them back at the Ashford police station.

"I thought you'd try to pull something like this," he said with a boyish grin.

"I cannot thank you enough for your prediction," Percy said, rubbing her wrists as the sergeant removed the cuffs. "I was just beginning to appreciate what a pickle I was in."

"That whole stunt has taken ten years off my life," Mrs. Appleby complained.

"We couldn't let you in on the ploy. It had to look authentic," said Percy.

"Authentic, is it?" the cook griped. "You're lucky you didn't have an authentic heart attack on your hands."

Percy patted her shoulder. "Please accept my deepest apologies, Mrs. A. I promise I'll make it up to you."

"Let's go into an interview room so you can debrief me," said Chief Inspector Thompson, gesturing with his arm.

The stark room was a blank slate with no windows, but it was clean.

As the inspector ripped off the blank canvas, Mrs. Appleby cried out. "You found it!"

"Yes," said the chief inspector. "In spite of the underhanded method, Mrs. Pontefract did manage to find the missing piece of evidence." He laid it on the metal table. "Now, let's hear what happened."

When the sergeant and Percy were done, she asked, "Have you heard back from the lab about the squirrel?"

The chief inspector huffed. "Not yet. But this forgery confirms that the Dowager Countess had a motive to kill Nigel. Think of the humiliation and frustration when they came to sell it only to be informed it was a fake."

"What happens now?" Percy asked.

"We have enough to arrest the dowager on suspicion of the murder of Nigel Fotherington. And I hope that by tomorrow, we will have confirmation that she attempted to murder you too."

"I would love to see her face," said Percy, whose blood was still steaming.

"Perhaps you can," said the chief inspector. "If she were to see you, alive, it would catch her off guard, making the arrest easier. Otherwise, I can see her putting up all kinds of resistance."

The dowager's family were staying at an upscale hotel while the auction was taking place. As Percy pulled up in a taxi, the sun shone on the whitewashed walls and shiny windows. She checked that Chief Inspector Thompson was secreted in the lobby and walked into the dining area where an extravagant dinner was in full swing.

Spotting the dowager, whose back was to the restaurant entrance, Percy took a wide sweep of the room, putting her directly in the old lady's line of sight. She was dressed in the same empowering outfit she had worn to the art exhibit and managed to walk without stumbling at all. Head high, slouch hat perfectly situated over trained curls, she pretended not to notice the dowager as she walked slowly past.

Out of the corner of her eye, she saw the elderly aristocrat start and stare, the already papery white of her skin turning a light shade of guilt gray.

Percy smiled as if she were meeting someone by the door, and the dowager turned to see who it was, coming eye to eye with the chief inspector. The dowager countess slumped.

The inspector's calculations were proven correct a second time. The dowager was so unnerved upon witnessing the ghost of Percy that she put up little resistance when arrested, though the same could not be said for the earl, her son, who wept and wailed and gnashed his teeth at the public indignity.

Percy had a front row seat to the whole satisfying show as the steely, villainous, old lady who had tried to kill her was propelled to the door of the hotel in handcuffs and placed in a police car.

# Chapter 21

Percy fell to the telephone seat in the cozy hall of her home with a bump.

"What did you say?"

"I said," repeated Chief Inspector Thompson, "that the dowager confesses to hitting Nigel over the head with the lead doorstop but is swearing with oaths that make me blush that she did *not* stab him."

*How could that be?* Percy felt the earth move beneath her.

"Mrs. Pontefract?"

"Yes, I'm here. It just doesn't make sense."

"I'm going to review all my other notes and see what I can come up with," the chief inspector continued.

"I-I appreciate you letting me know, Chief Inspector." The beeping of the phone line reminded her that she had yet to hang up.

Percy wandered into the kitchen like a sleepwalker.

"What's wrong?" asked Mrs. Appleby, tying an apron around her middle.

"It was the inspector. The dowager has admitted to hitting Nigel with the doorstop, but she insists that she did not stab him with the kitchen knife."

"Well, that's rather odd," commented the cook, taking flour out of a stone jar. "If she's admitted to the one thing, why not the other?"

"Because she's telling the truth," said Percy slowly. "Which means not only was Nigel killed in two ways"— she smacked the table so hard, Mrs. Appleby jumped out of her skin—"he was killed by two *different* people!"

"My giddy aunt!" exclaimed Mrs. Appleby, sinking into a chair. "Would you stop doing that!"

"Sorry! I just get so excited when the pieces start falling together," said Percy.

Shaking her head, Mrs. Appleby ran a work-worn hand down her face. "What an unlucky chap your cousin was."

Elbows on the table, Percy rested her face in her hands. "How will his family take all this?"

"Someone should write it down and sell it to Hollywood," said Mrs. Appleby. "It has all the trappings that people want; high society, the art world, love affairs, two murders—of the same person. I bet they've never seen the like. They're bound to buy it!"

The scraping of the chair legs on the slate tile floor made Percy wince as Mrs. Appleby made for the drawer and extracted the notebook.

"Time to go back to the old drawing board," she said, waving the book and plopping it in front of Percy.

She opened the notebook but stared into space. "This means that the dowager slipped down the back hall of the gallery, past the kitchen, grabbed the doorstop, whacked Nigel on the head and high-tailed it back, all while I was in my tipsy stupor. But unbeknownst to her, Nigel was not dead." She picked up the pencil and began to doodle. "Now we have to imagine another person, one who had also been burned by Nigel's illegal enterprise, attending the exhibition with plans to take their own revenge."

"Well, I never," murmured the cook, reaching for the butter. She cut it into small cubes and dropped it into the bowl, then began rubbing the flour and butter between her fingertips.

"However, the second person found him unconscious outside," continued Percy. "They must have checked to see if he was dead, but finding him to be breathing, took the knife they had swiped half an hour earlier, plunged it in and finished the job."

Mrs. Appleby's mouth pulled down and she rested a floury hand on the side of the bowl. "Incredible as it seems, I think you're on to something."

"Sir William," Percy murmured while writing his name in the book. "He lied to me about how well he knew Nigel. He knows art and is a sponsor of it. Could he be acting as a go-between for the forged paintings?"

Mrs. Appleby lifted her hands from the bowl, sending a shower of white powder onto the surface of the table. "What do you mean?"

"Could Sir William have been selling the fake art? He certainly has the credentials."

Pouring milk from a stoneware jug, Mrs. Appleby asked, "Is there a way of finding out?"

Percy sat thinking for a while, tapping her fingers against her lips. "Only if we can test him by presenting someone with pots of money who is eager to own something priceless," concluded Percy.

"Hmm. That is a problem." Mrs. Appleby began to knead the dough.

Percy bit the end of the pencil. "Unless we concoct someone. Play Sir William at his own game."

"But with Nigel dead, there are no more pictures," Mrs. Appleby pointed out.

"There is one: the forgery I found at Nigel's flat," declared Percy. "The chief inspector has it." She tapped the pencil against the scratched table. "Or, how about this? We set up a sting like I did in the last case. I'd have to convince Chief Inspector Thompson to go along with it." As she watched Mrs. Appleby roll out the scone dough, a scheme began to formulate in her brain. "I could call Sir William and explain that I was back at Nigel's flat and found an Old Master. I could act distressed and reveal that I don't know what to do about it as I fear it might be stolen and tarnish my cousin's reputation. Ask his opinion about what to do. After discussing the problem with him, I could say that I've decided to tell the police about it and will go to them the following day. This will put Sir William in a tight spot. If the painting is seized and sent for authentication, it will prove to be one of the forgeries which might lead them to Sir William. He will have to break into the flat and remove the fake to save his own skin. And we would be watching."

"What would that prove?" asked the cook as she cut out circles of dough and placed them on a cooking sheet.

"That Sir William knows where Nigel lives and was in cahoots with him all along. The papers haven't named Nigel as the forger yet and if this painting is found and valued, the game will be up."

"Ahh. But if Sir William *is* the accomplice why would he kill the hand that feeds him?" she asked, slipping the scones into the Aga.

Percy's shoulders slumped. "Oh, I hadn't thought of that."

"Who else is on the list?"

"Aunt Honoria and Uncle Frederick. I think they were absent for part of the time while I was dozing which means they could have been in the back alley with Nigel. But I cannot think of a motive. They do not go in for original art. Their home is filled with boring reproductions."

Percy flipped the page.

"Bernard Partridge, the praying mantis. He mentioned something to me about working on some forgery cases at the Old Bailey. He is certainly a social climber. Perhaps he heard there was an Old Master for sale on the black market for a steal and got burned. He may have exacted his revenge if he found out it was a forgery and his own brother-in-law was to blame. I doubt the newlyweds can afford to lose a large sum of money as he climbs the career ladder."

"How could you find out?" asked Mrs. Appleby

"A police search of his home?" She rubbed her nose. "I expect the chief inspector would need more to go on for such a search than a theory."

She turned another page. "Lord Banbury." The image of someone walking their dog near the house the day of the car accident came back to her. "He had that note. I wonder if the inspector got anywhere with the handwriting experts." She shut her eyes and thought back to the day of her cousin's murder. "He was awfully eager about staying with the body. Could have been a way of deflecting suspicion from himself."

"Gave him the opportunity to mess with things, too," said Mrs. Appleby. "Like removing evidence."

"Or planting it," suggested Percy, thinking of the jade stamp. "But what would be his motive?"

"The forgeries," said Mrs. Appleby.

"Yes, it keeps coming back to that, doesn't it? As long as none of the purchasers sold one, Nigel's operation was safe. But the dowager had considered it an investment to help save the estate."

"Could Lord Banbury have done the same? Bought one and then had the need to sell it?"

"That is certainly a possibility, but I have no way of knowing unless...bother! I think I'll need to call Mother again."

"Persephone!" cried her mother down the line. "I think I'm making progress."

"With what?" Percy asked.

"The fight against the road, silly! Isn't that why you called?"

It never ceased to amaze Percy that her mother could make herself the focus of any conversation. "Um, yes." She closed her eyes in pain as her mother launched into a detailed analysis of her machinations against her local government.

When Mrs. Crabtree began repeating herself, Percy butted in. "Remember I asked about Lord Banbury? Did you find out anything?"

"Funny you should ask. I was up at the big house for tea, and I dropped his name into the conversation."

Percy imagined that this was scandalously close to a lie. Her mother probably went to Marlborough House to ask them to sign a petition against the road and name-dropped the earl while at it.

"Lady Rogers asked me how I knew him, and I told her about the art exhibit, leaving out that the art was monstrous, of course, and the fact that Nigel had been murdered. She has very delicate sensibilities."

Percy wanted to snort out loud but kept control of herself.

"She told me her husband was related to him through marriage and wasn't it terrible that the poor man was laden down with death taxes."

Her mother carried on with her story, but Percy had stopped listening.

# Chapter 22

Percy wondered how Piers would feel if he knew she was in a police car at night, alone with a handsome inspector.

They were parked along the street from Nigel's flat waiting to see if Sir William would take the bait. Percy had called the inspector with all her ideas. He had informed her that Bernard was clean as a whistle, having been thoroughly investigated at the start of the case. Her aunt and uncle too. She had wanted desperately to ask him if they had investigated her mother but refrained, reasoning that he would have told her immediately if he had found anything dodgy.

On the other hand, the chief inspector had suspected that there was a death duties issue with the earl, since the estate he inherited was vast, and it was a problem plaguing every landed family in the nation. However, he had not been able to find specifics on the earl's finances as his accountant was a slippery chap who blocked his path and explained that his client had investments both in England and overseas. The financial chap had flashed some paperwork that certainly seemed to indicate that the earl was flush, and assured the chief inspector that all the earl's finances were exceptionally healthy.

The chief inspector wasn't totally convinced.

So, it came down to the two nobles, and Chief Inspector Thompson was more than enthusiastic about laying a few traps, starting with one for Sir William Packett.

Percy had begged to be able to come since she was the one who had suggested the idea. After some persuasion, he had agreed. Now they waited in the chief inspector's car with a thermos of hot coffee and some delicious buns made by her own, Mrs. Appleby.

"What did you actually tell Sir William?" she asked as she munched into her second bun.

"I told him that after a second search of Nigel's flat we had found what looked to be an original work of art from the 17th century. I asked if he knew anything about it."

"What did he say?"

"He's a very good actor," said the chief inspector. "Made a lot of non-committal sounds before saying he was as confused as I and had only seen Nigel's contemporary art. I laid the trap by telling him that since he knew nothing about it, I would be taking the painting to the National Museum first thing in the morning to have it valued."

"Nice."

"So, now we wait."

It was a clear night. The lights were out in the shoe store, and the high street only had streetlamps scattered every hundred yards or so, but the moon was bright, and if anyone came along, they would have a good view. Percy knew that other policemen were holding vigil in the back alley and another two in the flat itself.

"Tell me about yourself," she said, offering the inspector a cup of steaming coffee.

Chief Inspector Thompson shifted in his seat. "What do you mean?" By the inflection in his tone, one would think she had asked him to strip down and dance along the high street.

"You know, where did you grow up? Do you have any brothers or sisters? The usual." She had deliberately omitted asking about a wife.

"Oh." He relaxed. "Not much to tell, really. I grew up in Kingston and I have an older brother and a younger sister. My dad was a copper too." He took a sip. "What about you?"

"Well, you've met my mother…" She let the comment hang, and the chief inspector let out a little chuckle. "I have one younger brother, but we're not very close. He stayed away from home as much as he could when we were growing up, and I can't really blame him."

"Your father seems…quiet." He reached for a bun.

"Would you believe me if I told you he used to be the life of the party? Or so I've been told. Years of marriage to my mother have beaten him into submission."

"I actually feel sorry for the poor man—if that's not inappropriate." He took a bite of sticky bun. "I hope you don't mind me asking, and please tell me if I'm stepping over my bounds, but neither of your parents are particularly tall. Where did your height come from?"

"My granny. My father's mother," Percy explained. "She saved my life really. We were so compatible. It was hard for me when she died."

Taking another bite he asked, "And what about your husband? We've spoken on the telephone but I haven't actually met him."

"Piers is a civil servant, whatever that is supposed to mean. He travels a lot for work and is not particularly demonstrative, but when I had my accident, he was right there, holding my hand and fetching the doctor." An unexpected lump popped into her throat.

"I'm glad some good came out of it," the inspector commented.

"He's going to take me to Paris. Have you ever been?"

The inspector huffed. "Are you kidding? On my salary?"

"They say it's the city of love."

"Well, then I have no need—" The chief inspector's words were cut short as a shadowy figure came into view. "Game time." His demeanor transformed; he was all business.

Percy's pulse kicked up as they watched the figure in a dark coat, collar pulled up, and wearing a black hat, steal along the pavement.

"Should—" Percy began.

He held up a hand to stop her speaking.

164

The person did not hesitate, rounding the shoe store and going to the side door to the flat. It was harder to see what was happening in the darkness of the alley, but the door opened in no time, suggesting that the intruder had a key.

They looked up to the large windows of the flat. The swing of a torch beam danced along the glass as the trespasser searched for the final forgery.

Minutes passed, and Percy's stomach jiggled with nerves.

Without warning, all the lights came on and the place shone like a power station.

"That's my cue," said the chief inspector. "Coming?"

Percy dropped the bun on her skirt, cursing the icing that would, no doubt, adhere to the fabric, and splashing coffee onto her shoe as she hurried to put the little cup on the floor of the car. She wiggled the door handle and twisted her ankle slightly in her haste to exit the vehicle. The inspector was already across the road, and she ran to catch up.

From the bottom of the stairs they could hear a commotion as the police officers explained the suspect's rights. Out of breath, she fell into the bright room.

"Well, well, well," said the chief inspector. "I didn't expect to see *you* here."

# Chapter 23

As Percy straightened, her gaze collided with the clear blue stare of Lord Banbury. He was still resisting arrest.

"I have to say I'm surprised," said Chief Inspector Thompson. "I was expecting someone else."

"You have no right to arrest me," he growled through his irate mustache. "*I* am a peer of the realm."

"To me you are a common or garden murderer," the chief inspector replied.

"Murder! If you must charge me with something, it should be theft," complained the earl, fear replacing the bluster.

The chief inspector pulled out one of the rickety chairs from Nigel's table. "If you ask me, theft is just an act of desperation to hide your other crimes. No, mate, I'm charging you with the murder of Nigel Fotherington and the attempted murder of Mrs. Pontefract."

Lord Banbury dropped his vicious glare but remained silent.

"Let me tell you a story," the inspector began, crossing his legs. "A man inherits a great estate after his father dies and is laden with an immorally heavy death duty. He casts about for a way to pay for the taxes without having to sell the house and land. Through Sir William Packett, the strapped earl hears of an up-and-coming young artist who dabbles in modern art but has a promising talent for more traditional styles. He contacts the artist, and they form an alliance–a poor artist whose skills have not yet translated into cash and a new earl desperate to retain his ancestral home.

"Together they hatch a scheme to harness the artist's true genius and turn it into a fortune. The earl has an interest in art and is well known in those circles. He is considered quite the expert, in spite of what he told us to the contrary. He plants rumors in the right ears that certain Old Masters' works that have been in private collections for decades are coming up for private sale. He suggests that interested buyers can purchase the pictures under the table for far less than they would fetch at auction, and that the sellers are interested in a quick sale with no questions asked. How am I doing so far?"

If the earl were a dog, he would have tried to bite the inspector.

"I'll take that as an affirmative." The chief inspector grinned, and Percy sensed that he was thoroughly enjoying himself. She was still reeling from seeing Lord Banbury and not Sir William.

"With the earl's credentials and spotless reputation, they begin to hoist their forgeries on an ignorant and trusting public," continued Thompson. "The scheme works astonishingly well, and over a relatively short time, over a hundred forged paintings are sold to gullible aristocrats.

"After some time, I imagine Nigel becomes discontented with his share. After all, *he* is the genius behind the scheme. Without him there would be no forgeries. He likely demands a higher cut and threatens to stop producing the fakes. He may even warn that if the earl does not conform to his demands, he will inform experts that the industry had been flooded with fakes.

"But our earl is no idiot. He has succeeded in saving his estate and accrued a nice nest egg to boot. He has no intention of going to jail for fraud. He agrees to give Nigel a higher percentage to keep him happy but actually plans to kill him at the exhibit and put a stop to the whole thing.

"But when the earl goes into the alley to meet Nigel, he finds that someone has beaten him to it. Nigel is on the floor, blood gushing from a head wound. He kneels to check whether he is really dead, and when he discovers he's not, takes out the knife he picked up in the kitchen earlier and finishes the job. Then he rushes back inside and offers to 'protect' the body until the police arrive."

Though the earl refused to speak, fury and anger emanated from him. Percy could easily imagine him spitting at the inspector.

"Would you like to tell the dowager's story since you're the one that solved her part in the crime?" the chief inspector asked Percy.

Taken unawares, she felt her skin prickle with bashfulness. "If you don't mind."

"Not at all," said the inspector, gesturing with his arm for her to take the stage.

Percy brushed her wiry hair back from her face. "The Dowager Countess of Kent was in a similar situation to the earl. She needed funds. She heard from a trusted source that a famous piece of art was coming up for sale at a discount due to mitigating circumstances and distressed sellers. If she could just get her hands on it, she would be able to sell the painting privately for far more. It would solve all her money problems.

"She managed to borrow the necessary funds and secure the painting for a bargain. I imagine the dowager intended to sell it abroad to keep everything under wraps, but when she arrived at the appraisers, she learned to her horror that the painting was a high-quality forgery. Her financial burdens had now increased exponentially. Someone was going to pay for embarrassing her.

"I am sure she made it her business to uncover the forger and exact her revenge. After all, in the event she was caught, who would send an aging dowager to prison for murder? Then fortune smiled on her. An invitation to the counterfeiter's art exhibit arrived for her son. She couldn't believe her luck! Fate itself was validating her objective.

"Arriving at the exhibit as a wolf in sheep's clothing, Nigel had no idea that the dowager was a victim of his criminal activities. I imagine she watched like a hawk for an opportune moment, and when she saw him slip outside, she grabbed the door stop, hit him, and hurried back to the gallery as if nothing had happened. She must have been floored to hear Cecily declare that her brother had been stabbed.

"Then I began to poke about, and the dowager invited me to tea to see what I knew, and something I said made her nervous."

Percy was finding her stride and took the other seat at the little dinner table.

"But in a second stroke of luck, she heard I had been in a terrible car accident. After calling Agatha, she ferreted out that I had survived and decided to finish the job. After all, who would suspect poison after a person had sustained serious injuries in a car accident? It would be put down to some internal problem that had gone undiagnosed."

She turned to the inspector. "I think that's about it, but I do have one question. We told Sir William about the remaining painting. Not the earl."

The chief inspector twirled the hat between his hands. "Sir William and Lord Banbury run in the same circles. Sir William must have mentioned his conversation with me about the existing painting, and the earl thought his goose would be cooked if that picture was scrutinized by the National Museum and declared to be a forgery. Any policeman worth his sorts would eventually be able to link the earl to the crime. That about right?"

The earl growled and struggled against the cuffs.

"Get him out of here," said the inspector to the policemen. To Percy he said, "Well, that is a nice, neat and unexpected ending."

"What will happen? Nigel is already buried. Will there be an exhumation? Do the doctors have the know-how to declare whose strike actually killed Nigel?"

"Unfortunately, science has not progressed to that point; we will not be able to say if Nigel was going to die from the blow to the head when the earl stabbed him. It will make for an interesting fight in court."

# Chapter 24

Percy was sitting on the balcony of the hotel drinking café au lait with fresh, flaky croissants and drinking in the view of the Eiffel Tower. She felt someone snuggle into her neck.

"We should have done this a long time ago," whispered Piers, draping his arm around her neck and taking the seat beside her.

The trees along the Seine were in bloom, and the scent filled the air with a light fragrance she would never forget. "We didn't have the money," she replied.

Piers touched her lips with his fingers, sending a shiver up her back. "No talk about money…except to tell you that I was promoted and got a rise in pay."

"Why didn't you say?" she asked.

"I was saving the secret to surprise you on this getaway. I think we should be able to afford more treats like this in the future."

She let out a contented sigh.

Piers took a large bite of a buttery pastry. "I hate to talk about your cousin's death when we're spending a romantic weekend away but do the police know which one of the murderers cut your brake line?"

"On that score, the chief inspector and I were wrong. It *was* the dowager. Our conversation when she invited me over for tea made her extremely nervous. She found a slightly dodgy gardener who was happy to undertake the task for a hefty bonus. I had thought it was the earl because of the stranger walking his dog by the house, but the more I thought about it, the more I realized Apollo would have barked if he had sensed another dog on the property."

"You clever old thing!" He traced a finger down her nose, and her stomach did a somersault. "I think someone as intelligent as you deserves a new car, don't you?"

She sat forward. "Really?"

"Yes. Nothing too fancy and not brand new, but when we get back, we'll go shopping."

"Nothing will be like my old car." She smiled up at him. "Did you know I named her Lucille?"

"What, the car? No. You are funny." He pulled her close to him.

"She was a great companion."

Piers kissed her on the cheek. "And that old girl saved your life. I talked to Bob at the garage. The metal was such good quality that it didn't crumple. If it had…well." He smoothed her hair back from her face. "I don't want to think about it."

She turned her back to him as he wrapped his arms around her middle and kissed her neck.

"They have recovered over fifty of your cousin's forgeries," he muttered into her skin.

She twisted. "What? How do you know?"

He sat back slightly with a frown. "Saw it in the paper, I think." He pulled her close again.

*She hadn't seen anything about it, and she had looked.*

"He was truly gifted," she said. "It's a shame he wasn't recognized for it. The value of art is such a sophisticated business."

"A lot of artists only achieve real success after their deaths," he murmured. "Perhaps that will be the case for Nigel."

"I wonder. Agatha would not let me pay for that picture we have. When she learned of the part I played in finding his murderers, she insisted I keep it as a gift. And speaking of money, I couldn't understand why Nigel lived in such a modest place if he was earning so much from the forgeries. Turns out he had a secret bank account." Piers was running a finger across the top of her shoulders, making it hard to concentrate on anything.

"The seascape is an outstanding piece," he murmured.

172

"We will never know its value, as I will never sell it," she declared. "We shall hand it down to the children, and they will hand it down to their children. I shall insist."

A brightly colored boat floated by on the river.

"Shall we go boating today?" she asked as she felt her husband's breath tickle her skin.

He took her hand. "Let's save that for tomorrow."

*The End*

Thanks for buying my book!

Ann Sutton

I hope you enjoyed book 2, *Death is a Blank Canvas,* and love Percy as much as I do. If you have not read Book 1 yet, *Death at a Christmas Party,* is also available on Amazon.

https://amzn.to/43JXbrn

**A merry Christmas party with old friends. A dead body in the kitchen. A reluctant heroine. Sounds like a recipe for a jolly festive murder mystery!**

It is 1928 and a group of old friends gather for their annual Christmas party. The food, drink and goodwill flow, and everyone has a rollicking good time.

When the call of nature forces the accident-prone Percy Pontefract up, in the middle of the night, she realizes she is in need of a little midnight snack and wanders into the kitchen. But she gets more than she bargained for when she trips over a dead body.

Ordered to remain in the house by the grumpy inspector sent to investigate the case, Percy stumbles upon facts about her friends that shake her to the core and cause her to suspect more than one of them of the dastardly deed.

Finally permitted to go home, Percy tells her trusty cook all the awful details. Rather than sympathize, the cook encourages her to do some investigating of her own. After all, who knows these people better than Percy? Reluctant at first, Percy begins poking into her friends' lives, discovering they all harbor dark secrets. However, none seem connected to the murder…at first glance.

Will Percy put herself and her children in danger before she can solve the case that has the police stumped?

*Death at a Christmas Party is Book 1 in the new Percy Pontefract Cozy Mystery Series.*

I also write another cozy mystery series, The Dodo Dorchester Mystery series. If you are interested in a **free** prequel to that series go to https://dl.bookfunnel.com/997vvive24 and download *Mystery at the Derby.*

For more information about the series go to my website at
www.annsuttonauthor.com and subscribe to my newsletter.

You can also follow me on Facebook at:
https://www.facebook.com/annsuttonauthor

# About the Author

Agatha Christie plunged Ann Sutton into the fabulous world of reading when she was 10. She was never the same. She read every one of Christie's books she could lay her hands on. Mysteries remain her favorite genre to this day - so it was only natural that she would eventually write my own.

Born and raised in England, Ann graduated college with a double honors in Education and French. During her year abroad teaching English in France, she met her Californian husband. Married in London, they moved to California after her graduation.

Together with their growing family they bounced all around the United States, finally settling in the foothills of the Rocky Mountains.

After dabbling with writing over the years, Ann finally began in earnest when her youngest was in middle school. Covid lockdown pushed her to take her writing even more seriously and so was born the best-selling Dodo Dorchester Mystery Series. To date over 125,000 units have been sold or read on KU.

You can find out more about Ann Sutton at annsuttonsuthor.com.

# Acknowledgements

I would like to thank all those who have read my books, write reviews and provide suggestions as you continue to inspire.

I would also like to thank my critique partners, Mary Malcarne Thomas and Lisa McKendrick.

So many critique groups are overly critical. I have found with you guys a happy medium of encouragement, cheerleading and constructive suggestions. Thank you.

My proof-reader – Tami Stewart

The mothers of a large and growing families who read like the wind with an eagle eye. Thank you for finding little errors that have been missed.

My editor – Waypoint Authors

My cheerleader, marketer and IT guy – Todd Matern

A lot of the time during the marketing side of being an author I am running around with my hair on fire. Todd is the yin to my yang. He calms me down and takes over when I am yelling at the computer.

My beta readers – Francesca Matern, Stina Van Cott,

Your reactions to my characters and plot are invaluable.

Printed in Great Britain
by Amazon

25530959R00106